THE HAUNTING OF GREY HILLS

Distant Deep

JENNIFER SKOGEN

EPIC
Press

Distant Deep
The Haunting of Grey Hills: Book #5

Written by Jennifer Skogen

Copyright © 2016 by Abdo Consulting Group, Inc.

Published by EPIC Press™
PO Box 398166
Minneapolis, MN 55439

Cover design by Dorothy Toth
Images for cover art obtained from iStockPhoto.com
Edited by Melanie Austin

LIBRARY OF CONGRESS CATALOGING-IN-PUBLICATION DATA

Skogen, Jennifer.
Distant deep / Jennifer Skogen.
p. cm. — (The haunting of Grey Hills ; #5)
Summary: With the group is fractured, a long forgotten mystery may decide the
fate of the world, leaving Sam to find a cure for Jackson before it is all too late.
Meanwhile, an important figure from Trev's past resurfaces, forcing him to decide
once and for all where his loyalties lie.
ISBN 978-1-68076-033-0 (hardcover)
1. Ghosts—Fiction. 2. High schools—Fiction. 3. Supernatural—Fiction.
4. Haunted places—Fiction. 5. Young adult fiction. I. Title.
[Fic]—dc23
2015935809

EPIC
Press

EPICPRESS.COM

For my sister, always

Prologue

The voices were loudest up on the bluff, on a small patch of burned-looking ground where the trees wouldn't grow. As a child, Eli Grey would go up to the bluff—the farthest corner of his father's expansive property—and sit for hours. He liked to watch the distant waves and listen.

Eli couldn't always understand the voices. They were like a river that flowed around his mind, and every now and again something would catch. A woman who couldn't find her lost child, begging for help. A man who didn't know where he was. A child screaming.

The screams were the worst. On the days when

the screaming wouldn't stop, Eli would cover his ears and rock back and forth. When he could stand it no longer, he would leave the little clearing and run back home. He wouldn't go back to the bluff for days after that, sometimes weeks. The screams felt like someone was ripping out parts of his mind.

More often the voices just told him stories. Once a woman whispered that her husband had killed her, and the bastard had blamed her broken neck on a fall from her horse. The woman's voice sounded close to his ear, as though she were standing a few inches away from him. She asked Eli to find her husband and gouge out his eyes so he could no longer see the face of his mistress.

Another voice, a man's, would talk about the fire that was going to rise up and chew on the bones of the sinners. Eli didn't like this voice, but he couldn't help but listen.

Eli's father would slap him across the face if he mentioned the voices, but his brother, Kenneth, would listen to him. Kenneth couldn't hear the voices at first, but after a while he told Eli that he could hear the man who talked about the fire. Eventually Kenneth could hear that man even when they weren't in the clearing. Kenneth said that man wanted to save them.

Eli was nineteen when their father's house burned to the ground. Kenneth was twenty-two. They inherited everything.

Chapter One

"We can't just kill him," Sam said. She stood a few feet away from Jackson, who was tied to a kitchen chair. Jackson's face was covered with dirt and blood, and he watched her with a gaze that reminded her of a wolf. Calm, unblinking eyes. Gregory, Dom, and Trev kept looking back and forth between her and Jackson, as if they couldn't decide who was more dangerous.

Sam shifted from one foot to the other and held the icepack tighter to her swollen eye. It hurt like a bitch and was going to look incredibly ugly in a few hours. She'd had a black eye once before, and she remembered how everyone stared at her when she walked down the street.

One hour had passed since Jackson held Sam's face to the blue light. One hour since she had heard the voices crying out through the crack. Ghosts' voices. Just an hour, and Sam felt as if her whole life had rewound itself like an old cassette tape. She didn't know what song would play next, but she didn't think it was going to be one she liked.

Gregory sighed. "We don't have any more time, Sam. I can't destroy the ghost without killing him. If I had another option, I'd take it." Gregory was leaning against the kitchen counter, his eyelids drooping.

He looked exhausted. And not just an *I've-driven-all-night-and-could-sure-use-a-nap* kind of exhausted. Gregory had deep bags under his eyes that looked like shadowed half-moons and his hands were shaking. Sam wondered how much longer he could keep going like that. It looked as if any second he might just drop into a dead faint.

Whatever Gregory had done to subdue Jackson had taken almost everything out of him. Sam couldn't even imagine the kind of strength that had required. But then again, she could hardly believe that a ghost was inside Jackson right now, like a malignant tumor. Killing him slowly.

"And you've seen what he can do," Gregory continued, brushing his black hair out of his eyes. "I don't see another option. He's too dangerous to ignore, Sam. Surely you of all people realize that."

Sam kept expecting to hear sirens in the distance. She felt as though a great spotlight was going to shine in their window and SWAT teams were going to kick down the door.

"We just have to get him out of here," Sam said, trying to ignore how her throat ached with each breath, and how it was Jackson's hand around her neck that had made it hurt. "We just need to get him in the car and drive, and then we can figure it all out. But we can't stay here. The police are looking for him, Gregory. The police! That means they're going to find us, too."

Dom rubbed his shoulder. He was sitting in a chair across the table from Jackson. The impact of Jackson flinging Dom against the wall had done something terrible to his gunshot wound. Dom's voice sounded thick when he said, "I'm sorry Sam, but I agree with Gregory. It's our only option. I think it's what Jackson would have wanted."

"Fuck you, Dominick Vega," Sam spat. "Don't you dare talk about Jackson like that. Like he's already dead. He's right there. He can hear us."

Trev touched her arm. Sam winced and moved away. "This isn't easy for us," he began.

"Us?" Sam looked wildly between all three of the guys. "So you're all on the same side, is that it? You've all decided to just kill him and ask questions later?"

Gregory crossed his arms. He wouldn't meet Sam's eyes when he said, "What would you suggest? Just let this ghost, Eli, as he calls himself, keep eating your boyfriend from the inside out? Just let him keep killing people? This ghost is strong. He's the strongest I've ever seen. And I don't know how long we can hold him. He's going to get loose eventually, and then what? You saw what he did to Dom, to you . . . If you want to gamble with everyone's lives, well, I can't say I understand."

Jackson smiled at Sam but didn't speak. She remembered his voice when they were up in Dom's room—how it had sounded like Jackson, but also not. Who was this ghost that had snuck inside Jackson's skin? And if he was so powerful, why was he tied to a fucking kitchen chair?

"This isn't right," Sam said softly. Then, louder, "This has been too easy. Way too easy."

"Easy?" Dom scoffed. "He almost killed you." He paused, then added, "He killed Macy." Dom slouched in his chair as if his head was too heavy.

"He didn't kill Macy," Sam said, not taking her eyes off Jackson. That thing inside Jackson's head licked his lips. She refused to blink. Sam wouldn't let the ghost see her waver.

She moved the icepack to her left hand, then opened and closed the right one to let it thaw out. There had to be another option. Another way. Life wasn't this fucking narrow.

"Sam," Trev said slowly.

Did he think she was stupid? Was that what they all thought? *Stupid Sam doesn't understand*

what's happening, so we'd better make all the deci-
sions for her.

"I mean, this explains it," Trev continued. "Of course Jackson would blame her death on some other ghost. He's been possessed all along. He killed Macy, just like Dad killed—"

Sam whirled on him. "Don't you dare. This is nothing like Dad. He was still Jackson back then. There is no way he killed his best friend. He loved her. He would never . . . "

"Are you saying Dad didn't love Mom? Or Jamie?" Trev stared her down. "Of course, he did. But the ghost made him do it. And this ghost made Jackson kill Macy."

Sam looked to Dom and Gregory, and they just nodded their heads like those fucking toy bobble-head birds.

"So we just kill him?" she said. "And then what? Have you ever thought that this might be exactly what the ghost wants? He made it pretty damn easy to catch him. And now here he is, tied to a chair, just waiting for you to execute him? Now *that* is pretty fucking convenient."

Gregory sighed again.

He was a big sigher—she'd forgotten that about him. She'd also forgotten how fucking self-righteous he was.

"This is the only option, Sam. I'm sorry you can't see it, and I'm sorry this guy . . . Jackson . . . was your friend. But he's already gone."

"How do you know that?" Sam started to say, then coughed, pressing her hand to her throat. When she spoke again it was in a whisper. "He talked to me. Trev, you heard him, right? Jackson was talking to me right before he passed out. He said my name." Sam remembered the way he had looked at her when she held him in her arms. She knew it was Jackson. He was begging her to help him, to make the pain stop.

Gregory shook his head. "He was just saying what you wanted to hear, Sam. That's what they do."

"And you're the expert?" Sam said, then coughed again. Soon she was going to lose her voice completely. "How many other possessed people have you seen?" Sam asked. "How on earth do you know what they do or don't fucking do?"

Gregory was silent for a moment. He looked at Trev and then down to his shoes. "I've seen this before, okay?" Gregory finally said. "I've seen what a ghost like this can do. And keeping Jackson tied to a chair is not an option. Not even for another hour. Do you know why he's so strong? Why it took nearly everything I had to bring him down? He's not just feeding off Jackson. He was feeding off that blue light upstairs. That crack, as you called it. He's feeding off the other ghosts."

"Other ghosts?" Sam croaked. She remembered the voices she had heard when her face was inches from the blue light. The light that had been feeding off *her*. It had been sucking *her* dry. Did the ghost of Eli Grey do that to other people? To other ghosts?

"I've heard of that," Dom said, his voice was all scratchy, too. He put his hand on his shoulder again.

Sam wondered if anything broke when Dom's body was slammed against the wall. She felt a tad guilty at how little she had even really thought about Dom up to that moment. Sam wondered how many of his pills he had swallowed for the pain in the past hour. How out of it he was . . .

"Some ghosts are . . . amplified," Dom went on. "I think that's the right word. They're stronger when they're around other ghosts."

Trev took a step back from Jackson, who was still smiling. Sam tried to meet her brother's eyes, but he wouldn't look at her.

"Then how?" Sam said. "How are you going to do it? Shoot him in the head? Stab him? That's going to leave a lot of evidence. And it's not like you can just plead *ghost possession* as an excuse for murder."

Gregory started to say something but Dom cut him off.

"No," Dom said. "It's best if you don't know, Sam. You shouldn't have to picture it. I wish I hadn't seen . . . what happened. With Macy, I mean."

Sam wanted to slap him. "Fuck you and your broken heart. So you knew Macy, for what, two days? And now you're Romeo and Juliet?"

"Go to hell, Sam," Dom winced, and touched the back of his head. She hoped he didn't also have a concussion. Sam just didn't have time to worry about that too. "You don't know anything about it," Dom whispered. "You didn't even try to get to know her."

"Like you made any effort to get to know

Jackson? Do you think Macy would thank you for killing her best friend? No. If Macy was here she would be doing everything in her power to stop you, and you know it." Sam blinked away the tears that started to sting her eyes. She couldn't seem to catch her breath.

"Trev," she whispered, using up the last of her voice, "if you do this I will never, ever forgive you, do you understand that? And you'll never be able to forgive yourself." Her voice trailed off in a hoarse whisper, and she put her hand around her throat again. The skin on her neck was hot and tingled like someone had put stinging nettle on it.

Trev rubbed his eyes. "No, Sam. What I couldn't forgive is if we let him live, and he hurt more people. If he hurt you again." He looked at Jackson when he said, "You should go, Sam. Just go."

"He's right. We've got this, Sam." Gregory took a step closer to Trev. Her brother gave him a withering look and Gregory went back to leaning on the counter.

"Just go," Gregory said softly. "We'll call you when it's over."

So Sam went.

She walked to her room and got out the locked suitcase that she always kept under her bed, no matter where they were staying. She had started counting off the seconds in her head.

Ten seconds since she left the kitchen.

Fifteen seconds and she had entered the combination on the lock. Inside the suitcase were some clothes, a wallet with a fake ID, and ten thousand dollars in cash sewn into the lining. She also found a small plastic container that looked like a pencil box.

Thirty seconds and Sam opened the plastic

box. Inside were eight syringes full of a clear liquid.

Animal tranquilizer. After they were attacked by those two ghosts in New Mexico, Trev, Sam, and Dominick had broken into a veterinarian's office to fix up Sam's arm. Sam had helped herself to a few things.

One minute had passed since she left the kitchen. Sam walked back down the hall with the first syringe behind her back. She had never used one of the tranquilizers before, but she knew what a dose this size would do. She'd looked it up online.

Gregory was leaning over Jackson. He had a belt in his hand. Sam stumbled at the sight, her stomach dropping to somewhere below her knees. Gregory was going to strangle him. Were they planning to make it look like a suicide? *Poor, disturbed Jackson killed his best friend and then took his own life.*

Trev saw Sam first. He stepped in front of her.

His eyes were bloodshot. "Sam, just go. I don't want—"

Sam didn't let him finish. When she punched him in the face, Trev dropped like a fucking rock.

Chapter Two

Dom's car stalled as Sam was pulling onto the ferry. Someone honked behind her, and Sam resisted the urge to give the driver the finger. She took a deep breath and started the car, remembering to push in the clutch this time.

Why hadn't she practiced driving again after that day at the lake? It couldn't be that hard to drive a stick. People much dumber than Sam knew how to do it. Dom and Trev could drive a stick for fuck's sake. It was all about *feeling* the car, Trev used to say when he was teaching her. The car would tell you when to release the clutch.

All this car was telling Sam was that it was

suicidal because it kept dying. It was going to die and come back as a ghost car. Sam laughed out loud and groaned at how much laughing hurt her throat. Groaning hurt, too.

A ferry worker waved Sam up a ramp to the second level. She drove the length of the ferry and then down the ramp at the end until she was at the very front of the boat, looking out at the water. All that stood between her car and the waves was a thin piece of rope.

Another attendant put a wedge-shaped block in front of her tire, presumably so she wouldn't go flying off the ferry into the Puget Sound. A seagull floated in the air right in front of the boat, and Sam was pretty sure it was watching her. The bird tucked its wings and dipped down toward the dark water, and then out of sight below the lip of the ferry.

Sam thought that Jackson would stay knocked out for about two more hours. Three if she was lucky. She wanted to check on him, but she didn't know how to do it without someone seeing that she had a person tied up in the trunk of her car. That just wasn't a situation you could talk your way out of.

She really had to pee so, after triple checking that the car was locked, Sam walked up the stairs to the passenger area. She had found a pair of Trev's sunglasses in the car to hide her black eye, but she knew she must look terrible.

Sure enough, when she saw herself in the bathroom mirror it was like looking at someone who had come back from the dead, as if she had literally just pulled herself out of a fucking grave. After finally using the bathroom—thank God, because after a few more minutes in the car Dom might have needed to replace his driver's seat—Sam tried to do something about her appearance.

Her hair, which was sticking up everywhere in its hasty ponytail, was an easy fix. After finger-combing her hair and pulling it up into a more respectable bun, Sam went about wiping the dried blood off her chin and neck. There was absolutely nothing she could do about her face. It looked like someone had been using her as a punching bag.

The ferry ride across the Sound only took about a half an hour, but she could feel each second pulsing through her veins. What if there wasn't enough time? What if Jackson woke up too early?

Before she headed back down to her car, Sam bought a coffee from one of those vending-machine latte dispensers. It was too sweet. She wondered if Jackson would like it. Then she dropped it in the trash and walked down the stairs.

Chapter Three

Big cities were full of ghosts. That was one of the main reasons why Sam and the others usually avoided them whenever possible. Small towns were manageable. Or the empty, open road—that was the best. Just you and your car for miles and miles. No one who had lived or died. No memories. Nothing to run from or toward.

But cities . . . there was something about the density of people, and how their deaths just lingered. You could hardly walk down the street without running into a ghost. Sam and Trev were still living in New York City when they started seeing ghosts. Stepping out of their apartment was sometimes like walking into a fucking George Romero zombie movie. Zombies and ghosts weren't all that different, when you thought about it. Only, Sam supposed, zombies weren't real.

She couldn't actually remember who had seen the ghost first. Was it Trev? Sometimes Sam couldn't remember which events were her memories, and what was just something her brother had told her.

It happened just a few days after they found their mom and Jamie. A man was wandering the halls of their apartment building. He had killed himself a year earlier. Sam had remembered seeing him when he was alive, and she thought he looked almost the same when he was dead, only paler. Their neighbor had taken pills, she remembered her dad telling them. The man had just gone to sleep and never woken up.

Except, Sam had realized later, the dead man

had woken up. Was the afterlife anything like what he had expected? Did he wish he could kill himself again?

In the end, neither Sam nor her brother had ended up taking care of that particular ghost. They didn't know how.

They were still Trevor and Matilda Meyers back then, and Trevor and Mattie didn't know how to kill ghosts. Sam and Trev did.

When Sam changed her name, she chose Samantha because she'd always liked it, and she chose the last name Moss as a reminder: *A rolling stone gathers no moss.*

Sam was never going to stop moving.

Sam drove slowly off the ferry into downtown Seattle, car wheels thumping as they rolled across the ramp. She scanned the sidewalks. They were full of the living and the dead.

It wasn't always easy to pick out ghosts among a crowd. The pale girl on the corner about to cross the street, with the black Goth shirt and ripped jeans—was she alive? Would a ghost bother to look both ways before stepping out into the road?

Sam turned up a steep hill and almost immediately drove through a man who was just standing in the middle of the road. She was so sure he was a ghost that she didn't even bother braking. He had a bullet hole in his head, with a trickle of blood running into his left eye. Sam could also see right through him.

He glared at her before her car hit him, and she resisted honking her horn. She hoped all his ghostly pieces had scattered to the four corners of the wind when she hit him. She hoped not a single speck of him had reached Jackson in the trunk. Sam had no idea what might happen if the ghost inside Jackson found another ghost. Would he wake up? Would he bust out of the trunk while the car was still moving?

Sam didn't have a specific destination in mind, but she would know it when she saw it. She really should have done more research about Seattle, but it wasn't as though she had known she was about to stuff Jackson in the truck of Dom's car and drive to the city. That wasn't something you did if you had a real, thought-out plan.

Sam, Trev, and Dom had stopped in Seattle on their way to Grey Hills. They had spent an afternoon walking around some of the big touristy spots, like the Seattle Center with the Space Needle, and that weird-looking music history museum. They also made their way through Pike Place Market—that little collection of shops and booths that sold everything from piroshkies and used books, to smelly incense and glass hookahs.

Dom had insisted that they go see the fish vendors throw salmon through the air. Trev wanted to go to the original Starbucks (even though it had a long-ass line, and there was another, nearly empty Starbucks just a few blocks away). Sam thought her White Chocolate Mocha Frappuccino tasted exactly like any other White Chocolate Mocha Frappuccino from any other Starbucks in the world, but her brother had geeked out about it. He made them stand in front of the sign while another tourist took their picture. Trev was such a loser.

At the time Sam hadn't thought about Seattle as a place you could lose yourself in. Compared to New York or Los Angeles, Seattle seemed as compact as an oyster shell—the way all of the buildings were just huddled together on the edge of the water. You could practically hold the city in your hand.

Now she just hoped it was deep enough to hide them. She only needed a few days. A few days and she could find a way to save Jackson.

Sam watched the skyline, and drove toward the tallest, newest-looking hotel she could find.

That was the thing about cities. They were always growing. Always rebuilding themselves. Sam hoped that in a brand new hotel, no one had had a chance to die.

Chapter Four

Sam covered her hair with a baseball cap that she had just bought at a shop across the street. *Go Mariners!* She still wore Trev's sunglasses, and while she walked across the hotel lobby, Sam hoped that the security cameras were not aimed right at her. She didn't think that the boys would get the police involved, but for all she knew they might have told the cops that Sam was helping Jackson skip town. Sam might already be a wanted girl.

The woman behind the check-in desk had shiny brown hair and a too-white smile. The name *Leslie* was pinned to her blouse. "How can I help you?" Leslie asked in an overly cheerful voice.

Sam made herself smile back. "One room please. On your top floor, if possible." Leslie gave her a slightly quizzical look, so Sam said, "I like the view." The lobby was fairly busy, and Sam hoped that she would just be one more face in the crowd, if anyone happened to ask Leslie about her.

"Let's see," Leslie clacked away on the keyword for a few seconds. "Nothing available on the top floor—those are our suites—but we have a room on the 33rd floor. This room is facing the water, so you'll have a lovely view of the Puget Sound. How many days will you be staying?"

"Um . . . one week?" Sam said, hoping that would be enough time.

"We just require a credit card on file for incidentals." The woman must have noticed Sam's hesitation because she added, "And if you decide to extend your stay, that won't be a problem. You can settle your balance when you check out."

Sam couldn't use her usual credit card because Trev could probably find a way to trace it. For all she knew, a charge would show up online right away, and Trev knew all her passwords. Even the ones she hadn't told him. Hacking bastard.

So Sam said, "Actually, I'd like to pay up front. In cash." This wasn't a great idea either, because now Leslie with the shiny, perfect hair would remember her.

Sure enough, Leslie's eyes widened. "I'll have to check with my manager."

That was bad. A manager would definitely remember a problem guest. There might even be a record of it—"customer satisfaction" paperwork or some shit.

Sam made herself relax her shoulders. "Oh, that's fine." She reached into her wallet. "You see, the thing is, my husband doesn't like it when I use my card. I have a bit of a retail therapy problem. He's always saying that I'd just buy the whole store if he let me."

Sam lifted her sunglasses onto the top of her head, making sure that the woman got a good look at her black eye. "He likes me to pay in cash."

When Leslie averted her gaze, Sam continued. "But if you don't actually charge the card, then I don't think he'll mind. I don't think he'll be upset at all."

The woman sucked in her breath, then looked down at her keyboard and started typing. "Of course. Yes." Leslie nodded her head. "Actually, I think cash will be just fine."

"I can pay the full amount right now, of course. And put an extra $500 on my account. For any incidentals." Did harboring a possessed teenage boy count as an incidental?

"Of course," Leslie repeated, typing a few more things into her computer. "And, um, will you be staying by yourself?"

"Yes. I'm traveling . . . " Sam slid her sunglasses back down over her eyes, "alone." Then she handed a stack of twenties over to Leslie. "Keep the change. And thanks for your discretion."

Leslie nodded again, "If you need anything— anything at all—please do call the front desk." The woman looked like she wanted to take Sam's hand or give her a hug. Sam felt a little bad about pretending to be a domestic abuse victim, but she *did* have a black eye. And she *was* running from someone. Maybe she was a battered woman?

And now, if any of the guys came sniffing around here, Sam's new best friend Leslie wasn't going to tell them anything. She might even warn Sam, or Cassandra Nelson, as it now said on the account for her room, if anyone asked about her.

With her keycard in hand, Sam headed for the elevators. She always loved hotels. In a perfect world Sam would just live in a string of hotels until she died. One perfectly clean, nearly empty room after another with room service and cable. And a swimming pool.

Even after almost drowning in that duck-shit lake, Sam's skin practically tingled at the thought of diving into clear, cool water. Maybe she could inject Jackson with another tranquilizer and do a few laps later tonight. Although there were probably cameras everywhere in this hotel, and Sam in a bathing suit was not something people forgot easily, not to brag. Right now, however, with her body a patchwork of cuts and bruises, that was probably all they would really see. Swimming didn't seem so appealing after all.

The elevator had mirrored walls, and Sam kept the brim of her cap low over her face until she reached the thirty-third floor. Not only was she a little afraid of cameras, but she didn't want to see her reflection again. The hall smelled like lemons and fresh paint. When she slid her keycard into the door of her room, the little beep sent a flush of joy through her chest.

Home, she thought, opening the door.

Sam let the heavy door close behind her, and she jumped onto one of the two queen beds. She stretched out across the cool bedspread and made a little "bed angel" with her arms and legs. For five minutes she lay there, staring up at the ceiling, wishing that she never had to move again.

For the moment no one in the world knew where Sam was. She could be anyone. She could be *Sam*, or *Cassandra Nelson*, or even *Matilda* again, if she wanted. Beginnings, she had long ago decided, were the best place to be. Anything was possible.

Just one more minute, she pleaded with herself. *Just let me lie here another minute.* But there was no more time. Jackson might be waking up soon. And besides, she didn't really want him to smother in the trunk. Lord knew how much air was even in there.

If Gregory was right about Jackson's ghost getting his power from other ghosts, then Sam had to find a way to keep Jackson away from the dead. Up here, in the middle of the sky, there were no ghosts. What ghost would have a sentimental attachment to the thirty-third floor of a new building? What ghost would take the fucking elevator up here?

Before she went back to the parking garage, Sam took a moment to look out the window. Leslie was right: the room had an amazing view. Even though the sky was overcast, the lights from the buildings brightened the skyline. She could see all the way out to the Puget Sound, with the little, beetle-like ferries moving their passengers from shore to shore. From one life to the next.

Chapter Five

Two ghosts were loitering around the trunk of the car when she returned to the parking garage. Sam took care of them, but it exhausted her to do it without her knife. She just couldn't risk taking her knife out if she was being recorded, and for all she knew there was a security camera hidden right above her head.

She opened a granola bar she kept in her purse for this exact situation and ate it while leaning against the trunk. Taking care of ghosts, especially without using a weapon, always left her famished and weak. When she crumpled up the wrapper, the shaky emptiness in her stomach started to dissipate.

It wasn't going to be easy to get Jackson up to the room without looking incredibly suspicious. She couldn't exactly drag him up there. Or do some kind of *Weekend at Bernie's* scenario and prop Jackson up so it looked like he was walking on his own. But in the movie it had been a dead man, not someone zonked out on animal tranquilizers. *With a dead man inside him.*

Who was Eli Grey, really? The journal had told them practically nothing about him. And what right did Eli have to crawl his way inside her . . . not boyfriend, exactly. They'd never talked about it. It seemed like she and Jackson had talked about everything except how they felt about each other. And now Sam knew that the whole time she had been kissing Jackson, he'd probably had a ghost curled up in his brain, looking out at her. She shuddered.

Sam had considered getting a guest wheelchair and pretending that Jackson was an invalid. She could put a blanket over his legs, and everyone would just think he was sick or couldn't walk. But that would still draw attention, and people would see his face. Jackson could already be on the news if he really was a suspect in Macy's death. People might recognize him.

Sam was actually quite proud of the plan she had eventually come up with while lying in the heavenly queen bed upstairs. She wanted to send Trev a text, but, of course, she wouldn't. She didn't even have her phone—she had left that in her room in the yellow house, in case they could use it to track her. Sam was fairly sure there was an app that could do that.

Before coming back to the car Sam had found a luggage store a few blocks away and bought the biggest suitcase she could find. Even if money couldn't buy happiness, it could buy a whole lot of shit. And it could buy the best luggage to carry around your shit.

The most difficult part of her plan was going to be getting Jackson into the suitcase. After that it should be easy just to *roll* him up to their room.

As soon as she opened the trunk of Dom's car, Sam realized there was one hitch to her brilliant plan. The trunk was empty.

Chapter Six

Trev woke up on the kitchen floor. He had been lying on his arm, and so when he first tried to push himself up it was all pins and needles and useless. When he finally sat up his head went all foggy for a moment, and he thought he might pass out. His jaw was throbbing. It felt like someone had punched him in the face.

Oh yeah. That would be his sister.

Trev looked at his phone. It was a little past ten in the morning. He'd been out for more than three hours. Could a punch do that? He stood up, leaning on a chair as the room spun. An empty chair.

The same chair that Jackson had been tied to three hours earlier.

Oh, holy shit.

He spun around the room and saw the prone figure of Dom on the floor by the sink. Trev walked unsteadily over to his friend. Dom was breathing. Thank God.

"Dom?" Trev pushed Dom's shoulder, the one without the gunshot wound, and then lightly tapped his face. "Dom? Wakey wakey."

Dom's eyes fluttered, and he groaned. "What? Where . . . ?" He blinked up at Trev, his eyes not quite focusing.

"You're on the kitchen floor," Trev said. "And Jackson's missing. Sam's gone, too."

"How . . . ?" Dom sat up, then pressed his hand to his head. Trev was already looking for Gregory.

Gregory wasn't in the kitchen. Trev went into the living room, switching on lights. At first Trev didn't see anything, but then he noticed a pair of sneakers sticking out from behind the couch. He went over to Gregory, but didn't touch him for a few seconds. It had been so long since Trev had seen Gregory sleeping that for a moment it took his breath away. There was just the first soft shadow of stubble along Gregory's jaw. His eyelids fluttered—lashes so dark against his skin. Trev knelt down beside him and started to touch Gregory's cheek with his fingertips.

Trev squeezed his arm instead. "Gregory? Wake up now." At first Gregory didn't move, so Trev took his hand and pulled. "Time to get up."

Gregory's eyes flew open and he sat up. Trev scooted away from him and then stayed sitting on the floor with his back against the couch.

Gregory frowned, rubbing his forehead. "He's gone, isn't he?"

Trev nodded. His head felt strange, like his brain was made out of saltwater taffy that was still being stretched and pulled by one of those big machines.

"And your sister?" Gregory asked.

Trev nodded again, and then closed his eyes. It

wasn't fair. His sister wasn't supposed to be able to leave him, especially like this. Punching him in the goddamn face and drugging everyone. Putting herself in so much fucking danger because she didn't know when to let go.

Sam shouldn't be allowed to just disappear. Weren't twins supposed to have some sort of special connection? Shouldn't he be able to feel her, like she was a little glowing dot on a map?

"We have to find her," he heard Gregory say. "If she's hiding him, then she's fucked, you know that, right? And she's fucked us all. How could she be so stupid?"

Trev opened his eyes. Dom was standing over them.

"She's not stupid," Dom said. "We were. We left her with no other choice."

Gregory stood up. Trev had forgotten how tall Gregory was. Not that he was freakishly tall like Jackson, but he practically towered over Dom. When they were together, Trev had liked the way he could tuck his head beneath Gregory's chin and listen to him breathe.

Trev tried to push those memories down to whatever secret place in the back of his mind they were trickling out of. He didn't have time for this right now.

"We have to find her," Gregory said, holding his hand up to the side of his neck. Trev noticed a line of blood on Gregory's skin.

Trev glanced all around—at the floor, the couch cushions, the kitchen table. Then he saw it—in the shadows by the front door. An empty syringe. That must have been how she drugged them. Who the fuck did she think she was? Dexter Morgan, the serial killer from TV? *Jesus Christ!*

How many other secrets was she keeping from him? And how did she even know how to drug them like that? What if she'd done it wrong? What if she'd shot an air bubble into Gregory's neck and he just dropped down dead? Trev had read about that—that all you really needed to kill someone was an empty syringe.

"Shit," Trev muttered, realizing he had forgotten something big. He opened the front door and stuck his head out. Dom's car, which they had left parked on the street in front of the yellow house, was gone. Of course.

"Okay," Dom said after Trev reported the missing car. "Where would she go in three hours? If she hasn't already burned out my clutch or driven my car into a ditch?"

"Is there anyone she might go to for help?" Gregory asked. "Any friends in the area?"

Dom and Trev both shook their heads. "There was only Jackson," Trev said. "He's the only one who knew about all this stuff."

"Well, there's Claire," Dom said, pacing around the room. With his hair sticking up, and a nasty bruise forming on the side of his face, Dom looked a bit deranged. He rubbed his shoulder as he paced.

"But," Trev pointed out, "Claire and Sam

aren't exactly friends." That was putting it lightly. Claire was the main reason the police wanted to arrest Jackson. Claire had called the cops on him the night before and practically led the police to Macy's body. She had reacted surprisingly well to all the info they had thrown at her. It even seemed as though Claire had believed them when they mentioned ghosts.

Trev had been planning to talk to Claire about it today—to call her and explain more about, well, everything. But now he just pushed Claire back to the bottom of his mind. They had to find Sam. Everything else could wait.

"And now there's a *Claire*?" Gregory asked. His hand kept returning to his neck, scratching at the needle prick with his thumbnail. "You were just making all kinds of friends up here, weren't you?"

"Sarcasm doesn't suit you," Trev replied, digging his phone out of his pocket. Gregory was starting to look a little better. Maybe the *nap* had actually done him some good. He had some color back in his face, and his eyes didn't look quite so glossy. His eyes were lighter than he remembered, Trev suddenly realized. He thought they were more of an espresso black, but there were flecks of something in them. Gold and green.

Trev looked back to his phone. He did *not* have time for Gregory's eyes.

He thought about giving Claire a call, just in case, but he found himself pulling his sister's number up on his phone instead. He hesitated for a moment at her little icon photo. Sam's hand was out, trying to block Trev from taking her picture. She was laughing.

Trev pressed her number and held his breath. He heard it ringing, but it sounded strange, like there were two ringtones. Trev pulled the phone away from his ear a few inches, and he could still hear it ringing.

Trev's heart froze.

Sam's ringtone was coming from down the hall. From her bedroom. He held his phone away from his ear, but let it keep ringing as he walked toward her door. Gregory started to follow but Trev shook his head and motioned for him to stay back.

Trev didn't want to open the door. It was like Schrödinger's cat. He remembered their dad explaining the concept to them. The cat was alive and dead at the same time as long as no one looked in the box.

Sam was alive as long as he didn't open that fucking door. She would have laughed at him for comparing her to a physicist's hypothetical cat.

He closed his eyes and turned the handle.

When he opened the door he let out his breath. Sam's phone was sitting in the middle of her pillow like it was taking a nap.

Of course she would leave it here. Or course she would think of something like that—that Trev could find some way to track her if she kept the phone with her, as if this was an episode of *24*. Or maybe she just didn't want Trev to talk her out of this.

Whatever the fuck *this* was. Panic? A death wish?

I really hope you know what you're doing, Trev thought, picking up his sister's phone.

Chapter Seven

Sam stood perfectly still in the parking garage, watching the shadows around the other cars seem to pulse in the dim. Where was Jackson? She tried to feel him, to sense Eli the way she had back in Grey Hills. A dark, molasses feeling.

While she was driving with Jackson in the trunk of the car, she hadn't been able to feel Eli at all. But he had tricked her for God knows how long, so why would she be able to sense Eli now if he didn't want her to? Maybe it was something the ghost could just turn on and off like a fucking switch.

"Jackson?" Sam hissed, looking under Dom's car just in case.

She had no plan for this.

Jackson was supposed to stay asleep until she could get him upstairs and cuffed to the bed. Not in a kinky way. The handcuffs were another part of her special suitcase of wonders. She had felt like a secret agent when she bought them. To be honest, Sam had never really expected to use them. Ghosts don't exactly need to be handcuffed. But there were worse things than ghosts out there, and she wanted to be prepared for anything. That was the whole point of the suitcase.

It was her ticket anywhere. Her disappearing act.

Sam walked up the ramp, peering behind cars. She pulled another tranquilizer needle out of her purse and held it against her leg, hoping her hand masked it from view in case of any cameras.

"Jackson?" she said again. *Fuck, fuck, fuck.* Her arms were shaking. The granola bar wasn't enough.

A dark figure stepped around the side of a parked car, and Sam almost stabbed him with the needle before she saw that it was just another hotel guest.

Sam nodded to the man as he walked by, wondering how suspicious she looked in her dark glasses. She probably looked like a female Unabomber. Or—fingers crossed—just a college girl with a bad hangover. Once the man walked around the corner toward the entrance to the lobby, Sam resumed her search.

Why was she so sure that Jackson was even still in the parking garage? Maybe he was out on the street already. If he got out there she'd never be able to find him. The cops would probably find him first, and then all hell would break loose. Literally. Who knew what kind of damage Eli could do in a city full of ghosts?

It was too dark with her sunglasses on. Sam pushed them up on her head. In that instant, she saw a movement out of the corner of her eye. She swung around.

Jackson was standing right behind her. He was smiling.

Sam threw her sunglasses at him without thinking. They both watched the glasses bounce off his chest and break apart on the cement.

"Is that the best you can do?" Jackson asked. No. It was Eli talking. Sam had to keep reminding herself of that. He was glowing, she realized—a faint bluish haze surrounded his arms and his head.

"Why don't you step a little closer and find out," Sam said, making herself smile. She put her hand with the needle behind her back.

Jackson . . . no, Eli . . . shook his head. "So you can prick me with that little needle again? No. I think I'll keep my distance this time." He raised his hands, and the blue light grew brighter. The air between them started to crackle, and the loose hair around Sam's face started to float around her head like she was touching a goddamn Van de Graff generator. Her left eye twitched.

And then pain.

Sam couldn't even scream. It spread out from

the center of her—maybe her heart, or her lungs— as though all of her nerves and veins were on fire. She couldn't breathe.

Sam dropped to her knees, covering her head. She had been wrong. She should have just let them do it. Let them kill Jackson. Anything to stop the pain she was experiencing now. Anything . . . anything would be better than this.

Sam squirmed on the ground, pressing her face to the rough, cold cement. The pain was endless. Why wouldn't he just kill her? She tried to speak, but her teeth were clenched shut.

"You made me do this," Eli said. He didn't even sound like Jackson anymore. "Do you think I want to waste my energy on you? But you *had* to keep trying to save him. He's gone, don't you see that? This body—this Jackson you knew before—is gone. It is *my* body now."

Sam could see his shoes—his old, muddy Chucks—inches from her face.

"Just a few more seconds," Eli said from

somewhere above her. "Then it will all be over. Not even your ghost will be left."

Somewhere through the endless pain Sam heard the roar of an engine. Then there was a loud *thump*. Jackson's shoes lifted out of Sam's line of sight.

All at once the pain stopped. Sam could breathe. She flung herself onto her back, taking in huge gulps of air. As she stared up at the cement ceiling, a face appeared above her.

It was Claire.

Chapter Eight

"Are you okay?" Claire was saying, but Sam could hardly hear her. Sam's ears felt like they were full of cotton.

Sam nodded as she opened and shut her mouth, rubbing her jaw. It hurt from having her teeth clenched. The air smelled funny, like iron, or blood. Was it her blood? Or did it have something to do with Jackson's glowing arms, and that freaky electric crackling she had heard. Could she smell *him*? Eli?

Claire pulled on Sam's arm. "Come on," the girl said, her voice fast and frantic. "You have to help me. I think I killed Jackson."

Oh fuck. Jackson. Sam had been so relieved that the pain was gone that she hadn't really thought about *why* the pain was gone.

"What did you do?" Sam asked. Her voice still sounded hoarse, as though the words were catching and scraping on her throat on their way out.

"I fucking hit him with my car, okay? Come on." Claire pulled Sam all the way up and dragged her to the crumpled form in front of her blood spattered VW Golf. "Is he alive?" Claire asked, pushing Sam toward him. She seemed to think Sam was a doctor and not just a junior in high school. A junior who was actually old enough to be a senior but had skipped too many classes over the years and so was probably actually dumber than most sophomores.

Sam tried to focus, but her mind was spinning like a hamster wheel.

"You hit him?" Sam finally asked. While she was writhing in pain, Sam had wished that Gregory had just killed Jackson. But seeing his body splayed out on the ground—his arm flung at a strange angle behind his head—Sam could hardly breathe.

Claire pushed Sam again. "Come on. He's either alive or dead, but we have to fucking move." Her voice was calmer, more matter-of-fact. "We should get him in my car. Someone might come along any second now."

Sam nodded, but still had trouble making herself go any closer to Jackson. What if he wasn't really hurt? What if Eli was faking it and he leapt up and his arms started to glow again? What would she do? The memory of the pain was so real it felt like a phantom limb. She couldn't move.

Then Claire was tugging on Jackson's legs. "Come on. I can't lift him by myself."

Before she moved Jackson, Sam found her syringe and injected him in the neck. Just to be safe.

Then, together, they put Jackson in Claire's car and drove to where Sam had left the giant suitcase. While she was helping Claire lift Jackson out of the backseat of the Golf, Sam realized that no one had told Claire about Jackson—that he was possessed. Why the fuck had she hit him with her car if she didn't know that a ghost was inside him? Had Claire thought she was just running down Jackson? *Bitch.*

Sam decided that could wait. There were too many things to do before she and Claire could have a heart-to-heart.

As gently as they could, they curled Jackson's unconscious body into the suitcase. His legs were so long that Sam almost couldn't fasten the zipper without having a foot sticking out. Somehow they managed. When Sam tried to roll the suitcase, it was surprisingly light. Jackson really was quite skinny.

And alive. Jackson was still alive.

Sam had found a strong pulse, and his breathing

was even. She didn't know what parts of him were broken, but she couldn't do anything about that now. It wasn't as though she could take Jackson to a hospital. Just imagining the number of ghosts that would be there, ready to offer Eli their power, made Sam sick to her stomach. No, no hospitals.

Sam didn't know what to do about Claire's car, so she handed her a few twenties and told her go drive it through a carwash. "Then park it somewhere—up on Capitol Hill or somewhere residential. Somewhere where you won't get a ticket if you're parked for a few days. Take a taxi back here. Pay for everything in cash. Just come back here when you're done. We'll figure out what to do when you get back. I'm in room 335."

That had been Sam's original plan for herself—to go park Dom's car somewhere, so if Dom and Trev did report it as stolen it wouldn't be traced to this hotel. She'd have to do that later, after Claire got back.

Claire's eyes were narrowed, and her lips pressed

tightly together. Finally, she nodded. "But if you're not there when I get back," she said, "I'm calling the cops. Deal?"

"Okay, deal," Sam said, realizing that she had never given Claire a second thought until today. Until the last few minutes. Not really. Not when it might have made all the difference. What if they had told Claire everything from the beginning? Claire had known that something was different about Jackson. That something was wrong. Maybe they could have figured it out together.

Sam shook such thoughts from her head. There was no room for *what if*s.

Chapter Nine

Sam felt as if everyone was watching her as she walked through the lobby toward the elevators. *Nothing to see here. Just a bleeding boy in a suitcase. No big deal.*

When the elevator doors finally closed with her and Jackson inside, Sam let out a deep breath. Then she saw him.

There was the ghost of a middle-aged man standing right beside her. He looked like any other normal person who was just waiting for the elevator to reach his floor, except that half of his head was gone. She could see his brain, gray and mottled, through a huge crater on the side of his head.

She took out the knife—Macy's little butterfly knife that Sam hadn't been able to bring herself to throw away—and stabbed the ghost in the throat. A raw, primal sound escaped through her lips. The ghost reached his hands toward the knife, which was still firmly gripped between her fingers. Then he disappeared. She could feel it happen: a tightness in her chest that suddenly released. A fist letting go.

Sam glanced up to where she thought the camera might be, keeping the brim of her hat low over her eyes. She just had to pray that no one would look at the video. Hopefully this camera, and any that might be in the parking garage, was just on a loop and rerecorded over the tape every few days without anyone watching the footage. If she was lucky, any trace of her would be wiped clean in forty-eight hours.

It was harder than she ever thought possible to move Jackson from the suitcase to the bed, but

Sam managed it after a few tries. He was just so dang floppy, like a huge ragdoll, or some kind of human slinky. When she hoisted him by his shoulders up to the bed, he let out a sad little moan.

Whatever Claire had done to him when she hit him with the Golf must be hurting him. Sam was afraid that she'd made it worse—what if he had a broken rib and she punctured his lung when she moved him? What if Jackson was bleeding to death right now?

The metal bed frame seemed sturdy. She hoped the handcuffs would hold him. If this plan was going to work—if it even was a plan—then she needed Eli to wake up. She needed to question him.

So she needed Gregory to be right. If there were no ghosts around for Eli to feed off, then he shouldn't be able to use his freaky blue electric power. There were far too many *if*'s in her plan.

Sam pulled a chair up to the side of the bed. Jackson's brow was furrowed, and there was a smudge of blood by his mouth. It looked like his lower lip had split open. *Now they matched*, Sam thought grimly, feeling her own cut lip with her tongue.

She got a damp washcloth from the bathroom and wiped away the blood from his lip and then washed the rest of the dirt from his face. Then she lifted his hands, one at a time, and washed those as well. There was something dark beneath his nails that wouldn't come out.

Sam turned on the TV while she waited for Claire to return. She flipped through a few channels before she found the news. Rain tomorrow. Rain or snow the next day. Sam waited through a few stories on gas prices and foreclosures (she was really starting to miss the mindless games on her phone) when she heard the words, *Grey Hills*. Macy's picture was on the screen. Then Jackson's face was on there, too.

Sam looked over to where Jackson lay on the other bed and saw that his eyes were open.

"I didn't kill her," Jackson said. He didn't sound angry, or cruel, or mocking. He sounded like Jackson.

Sam picked up the tranquilizer and walked back to the bed.

"Did Eli kill her?" she asked him, still keeping her distance. It would be so easy to reach her hand out and lay it on his chest. To feel his heart beating.

Jackson frowned. "I already told you. Jackson's gone. I *am* Eli."

Sam's face crumpled. She turned away for a moment, holding her breath so she wouldn't scream. Then she took a step closer and jabbed the needle into his neck.

Just before his eyes closed all the way, Eli murmured, "Henry killed her."

Sam wanted to take back the tranquilizer and

hear what he had started to say, but it was too late. For better or for worse Jackson was asleep.

She turned off the TV. While she waited for Claire to come back, Sam watched her reflection in the window. She looked like a ghost herself.

Chapter Ten

Sam wasn't sure how she fell asleep. After a day of sitting around the hotel room, alternating between watching Jackson sleep, trying to question him (unsuccessfully) when he woke up, and then drugging him up again once she and Claire were too unnerved by his creepy smile, Sam was exhausted. But the idea of sleeping in the same room as Eli gave her the fucking creeps.

When she woke up, Sam saw someone standing in the corner of the room by the window. Sam sat up. It wasn't Claire.

Claire, who had the first watch, was still sitting

by Jackson's bed looking at her phone. Her face was lit with the soft, white light.

"Go back to sleep," Claire whispered, glancing up from her phone. "It's only been about an hour. I'll wake you at two, like we said." Sam nodded, her eyes still on the figure behind Claire.

It was Macy.

Macy stepped closer to Claire, then put her finger up to her own lips. "*Shhh*," Sam could almost hear Macy say, but not quite. It felt as though Macy's voice was lodged somewhere deep in the back of her brain. Sam could feel it, but not really hear it.

Macy stroked Claire's head. Claire shivered once, but didn't look up from her phone again.

It was too dark to see if Macy looked the same as the last time Sam had seen her. Her throat sliced open. Blood staining the front of her dress a shade darker than her red cape. Her lifeless, bare arms.

Sam never wanted to see her like that again.

Help him, Sam heard Macy say. *Help Jackson.* Then she was gone.

Sam didn't sleep again that night, but just lay there staring up at the dark ceiling until Claire shook her at two a.m. "My turn," Claire said, climbing into bed next to Sam. "Don't let Jackson kill me in my sleep, okay? Promise?"

"Pinky swear," Sam said, throwing her legs over the bed. Then Sam turned on the light while Claire squeezed her eyes shut and pressed her face into the pillow. Sam took one of the remaining tranquilizers out of her purse. Then she slid the needle into Jackson's neck.

They couldn't keep him doped up forever (who knew what it was doing to Jackson's already battered body), but Sam needed the rest of this night to get her bearings. She needed to figure out an actual plan and not just keep reacting to each shitty obstacle that was thrown in her path. Sam needed to figure this all out because, otherwise, it wasn't just Jackson who might end up dead. If Eli Grey got his way, it could be the whole fucking world.

Sam could still see the light from the crack in Dom's floor when she closed her eyes. What was Eli planning? What were the cracks supposed to do? Was Eli planning to keep ripping holes in the world until there was nothing left?

The hours went by slowly. Sam thought about how unlikely it was that Claire had even ended up in Seattle. After Claire got back to the hotel, she had told Sam why she was there.

"I followed you," Claire said, not really taking her eyes off the unconscious Jackson in the next bed. "I was still outside your house when Jackson showed up, and I waited. I didn't know what to do. And then, eventually, you came out dragging Jackson and stuffed him into the trunk of your car. So I started my car and tailed you. When you got on the ferry I completely freaked out. I was like, *What the fuck am I doing?* I had to pull off to the side of the road and sort of hyperventilate into my purse for a while. I almost missed the ferry, and then I couldn't find you. I almost just called the police."

"Why didn't you?" Sam had asked.

Claire stared at Jackson and absently placed her fingertips to the middle of her chest. "You won't believe me."

"Are you kidding me? Do you think there is a single thing I wouldn't believe by now? If you tell me that aliens beamed down into your car and told you not to call the police, I'd believe you."

Claire scrunched up her face. At first Sam thought she was glaring at her, but then she realized that's what Claire looked like when she was trying not to cry.

"I heard Macy, okay? I heard her voice tell me to follow you. That you'd need my help. She told me to drive to this hotel, and then to step on the accelerator when I saw Jackson standing over you in the parking garage. I could almost feel a hand on my leg, pushing my foot down on the gas. But that's crazy, right? I mean, Macy's not really here. She's not coming back. I know you said all that stuff about ghosts, but . . . " Claire trailed off.

She looked up at Sam with her gigantic blue eyes. Sam could tell that Claire wanted her to tell her that yes, it was possible. That Macy was still here. That she was still *alive*, in some fashion.

Sam hadn't told Claire what she wanted to hear then. And now, in the middle of the night—while she watched Jackson's motionless form in the dark—Sam knew she would never tell Claire. Because what Sam was doing in the dark was waiting. Waiting for Macy to come back.

Waiting wasn't exactly the right word. Sam was dreading it. If Macy came back, Eli might be able to feed off her energy, or whatever it was that he did to grow so powerful and glow like a jacked-up lightning bug.

If Macy came back, then Sam was going to have to destroy her to keep her away from Jackson. So Sam really, really hoped Macy would stay away—wherever *away* was. If her plan (the plan she had been forming during the long hours before sunrise) was going to work, then Sam couldn't have Eli gaining any more power from a ghost. Especially a ghost who used to be one of the strongest people Sam had ever met. Macy had been able to take care of ghosts like she was flicking lint off her sleeve.

So, no, she wasn't going to tell Claire. She wasn't going to bring Macy back into her friend's life only to destroy her again.

Sam liked to think that she might not be able to do it—to destroy Macy. She wanted to be that kind of a person, someone whose heart wasn't a cold, hard stone. But deep down she knew that wasn't true. If Macy came back, Sam wouldn't hesitate.

"Stay away, Mace," Sam whispered into the darkness. "Don't come back. I don't want to watch you die again."

Chapter Eleven

"Isn't someone going to be looking for you?" Sam asked Claire the next morning over breakfast. They had ordered room service and covered Jackson with a blanket when they opened the door, just in case. Sam ordered pancakes, sausages, eggs, and a mimosa (the Cassandra Nelson on file was twenty-two years old). Claire had granola with skim milk and coffee. Black.

Claire shook her head—her long, blond hair catching the light. It was actually starting to look a bit greasy. Sam didn't think she had ever seen Claire not looking completely immaculate.

"Mom thinks I'm at Dad's house," Claire said.

"And I told Dad that I needed to go to this special counseling retreat, for, like, grief. I told him that I didn't want Mom to know about it—that I'm in 'too fragile a place right now,' so he's covering for me."

"Your dad actually bought that?" Sam asked, "A 'counseling retreat'? Didn't he want to know where, and with who? You know, normal parent questions?" She finished off her mimosa in one long gulp. Sam wanted to order another, but decided she'd better keep her head clear for the day ahead. She'd drink a bucket of champagne when this was all over. She'd take a fucking bath in it.

"My parents hate each other, and I've never lied to my dad before. He bought me my first box of condoms when I told him I wanted to start having sex. And he didn't tell my mom about that either." Claire dug into her granola.

"Jesus," Sam said, shaking her head. "My dad

would have flipped if I had even said the word *sex* in front of him."

"Dad wasn't too happy, but I asked him if he wanted me to have sex and get pregnant or maybe AIDS, or if he wanted me to be safe. So he bought me some condoms, and took me to get on the pill."

"Why didn't you ask your mom?"

"I live with my mom—I didn't want her thinking I was out having sex every time I went on dates. And she's a bitch."

When Jackson made a soft groaning sound, Sam and Claire jumped up off their bed. "Shit," Claire said under her breath. Then, "What's the plan if he, like, busts out of those handcuffs?"

"He's not going to," Sam said.

"How do you know?" Claire didn't take her wide eyes off Jackson for a second.

Sam edged closer to the other bed. "Because if he does, I have no fucking plan, and we're probably going to die. Because I can't stop him. So he's not going to."

"You're not really making me feel better." Claire grabbed her purse and pulled out her phone and some pepper spray. "I'll just have these handy."

Sam almost laughed. It was six-thirty in the morning, Claire was still in her little snowman pajamas, and she had *pepper spray* in her hand.

"Okay, Claire. *You* can protect *me* if he gets loose."

Sam went over to Jackson and checked his handcuffs. They still seemed tight, and the metal bed frame appeared to be holding. As Jackson's eyes started to open, Sam realized yet again how ill-prepared she was for kidnapping anyone, let alone some old-timey ghost in her boyfriend's body. *Was Jackson her boyfriend? Did that in any way matter right now? Jesus Christ.*

Sam made herself get back on track. This was what sleep deprivation did to a person. She was too busy thinking about her relationship status when what she really needed to figure out was how she was going to feed him. Or let him use the bathroom . . . They could just let Jackson wet the bed, but that certainly wasn't an ideal solution.

"Jackson?" Sam said softly.

"I told you," came a throaty whisper. His eyes were still closed. "He is not coming back. However, unless you'd like his body to die, perhaps you could give me some water?"

With Claire standing at the ready with the pepper spray, Sam took a bottle of water and carefully poured some into his open mouth. He drank half the bottle, then started coughing.

"How do you feel?" Sam asked. "Does anything hurt?"

Jackson coughed again, then shook his head. "Everything hurts. But I don't think anything is broken if that's what you're asking. He has a nasty cut on the back of his head, and there will certainly be some fairly extensive bruising. However, I do believe we'll survive. That is, if you'll be so kind as to feed us something."

Sam gave Jackson the rest of her eggs and sausage, feeding him at arm's length with a spoon. Then Sam held the empty water bottle while Jackson pissed into it. Claire looked down. Jackson smiled at Sam while she carried his pee away.

Eli thought he could humiliate her, but that was not going to happen. And Sam was definitely not going to unlock those handcuffs so he could walk to the bathroom. She had no idea how to handle it if he had to do anything else, but they'd just cross that bridge when they came to it. Sam poured the pee into the toilet, then washed out the bottle. They might need it again.

Sam took a shower while Claire kept watch over Jackson. She turned the water up so hot that her skin turned a bright, raw-looking pink. Sam stayed in the shower longer than she had intended, just letting the water wash over her shoulders and back while she watched it go down the drain. Long clumps of her hair went with it. Jackson must have ripped it out when they were struggling the day before. Eli. It was Eli, not Jackson.

Sam had to keep telling herself that because it *was* Jackson. It was his face, and his hands. He was still in there, somewhere.

"Fight harder," Sam whispered, barely audible over the water. "Keep fighting."

After Claire took a (much quicker) shower, Sam put her hair back up in the baseball cap and slipped on her sunglasses (she was able to push the lens back in the frame after it had popped out. Good as new).

"Claire, I have to go do something," Sam said, picking up her purse and heading for the door. "Stay here and keep an eye on him for a few hours?"

"Are you kidding me?" Claire crossed her arms and walked to the door. "You're *not* leaving me with him."

"Someone needs to watch him."

"Then you stay here. Tell me where you were going and I'll go instead." Claire was only halfway through putting on her makeup, so one of her eyes looked bigger than the other. She kind of resembled a Picasso painting.

Sam shook her head. "I have to do this."

"Then drug him back up and take me with you. I'm not staying with him."

"That's not a good idea."

"Well, I'm not staying. I'll go wait in the lobby as soon as you leave. I'm not letting this fucker kill me. That is *not* how I'm going to die."

"Do you have a preference? For dying, I mean?" Sam asked.

"Yeah," Claire said, holding the eyeliner up to her other eye, "old age."

In the end Sam gave Jackson one and a half

tranquilizers and hung the Do Not Disturb sign on the outside of the door. She wondered how long they could go without housekeeping coming in and finding Eli. Maybe she could put in a special request at the front desk since she was such good friends with Leslie and all.

As she and Claire got in the elevator, Sam just had to hope that she had hit that sweet spot between overdose and the tranq wearing off too soon. She should have spent more time learning useful things like that instead of watching bad television. But it was *Dexter* that had given her the idea for the animal tranquilizers, so maybe TV really was the answer to life's problems after all.

It was raining outside—a cold, almost-snow that kept almost getting in her eyes. Sam had been planning to catch a bus, but Claire called them a taxi.

"I think there are cameras on buses," Claire said. "And besides, do you really want to ride a city bus? Gross."

Sam gave the taxi driver an address about two blocks away from their real destination. As they sped off through the rain, Sam wondered if her brother had figured out her plan yet.

Chapter Twelve

Where would you go if you were hiding from your own twin? Trev had spent the night trying to decide just that. Dominick wanted to report his car stolen and have the police track her down, but Trev told him to wait a day.

"She might call," Trev said.

"She's not going to call," Dom countered, holding up Sam's phone.

"There *is* such thing as a pay phone or a hotel phone. Or she could borrow a stranger's phone."

Dom shook his head. "She's trying to save Jackson's life. She's not going to call if she thinks we might kill him."

Trev and Dom were alone for the time being. Gregory was out inspecting the crack by the old bunkers. Trev thought Gregory really just wanted to be alone while he processed what on earth they were going to do next. Trev, for one, had no idea what else Gregory might have planned.

If it could just be Gregory . . . but that was always going to be the problem. Gregory was part of a package deal. Wherever he went, the Wardens were sure to follow. The Wardens . . . Trev wondered if he and his sister would ever truly escape them.

"Then what do you suggest we do?" Trev asked.

"Um, go find her? She's in real danger." Dom had Sam's phone and was absently turning it off and on. "Jackson is a time bomb."

"We can't just leave the cracks unmonitored. What if something happens and we're not around to stop it? What if a fucking army of ghosts pours out or something? And we're just wandering around the countryside looking for my stupid sister? We don't even have a car."

"Greg has a car," Dom said.

"Gregory."

"What?"

"He doesn't like it when you call him Greg."

Dom scoffed. "Well, you know how many fucks I give about what Greg wants? I'll give you a hint, it's somewhere between zero fucks and negative-one fucks."

"He's just trying to help."

"Less than zero fucks, remember?" Dom turned on the phone again, staring at the screen. "Hey, what's your sister's password?"

"I don't know."

"If you had to guess."

"Um, 'fuck off'? Or 'fuck you stop trying to guess my password'?"

"That's way too many characters." Dom started typing in a few things, but Trev reached out his hand.

"Give it back. She'd kill me if she found out I let you mess with her stuff."

Dom rolled his eyes. "I think she lost any privacy rights when she stabbed me with a needle and stole my car." But he handed over the phone.

They waited in silence for a while, Trev sipping the last of the whiskey straight from the bottle and trying to figure out how to get into Sam's phone. Then Dom disappeared upstairs. He was still trying to make a Token to bring Macy back, which was just too messed up to even contemplate at the moment. You couldn't just bring your dead girlfriend back to . . . not quite life. Afterlife?

Trev had gone through Dom's room after he noticed an aura of secrecy that seemed to ooze off Dom like it was some kind of fucking metaphorical Axe Body Spray.

The thing was, after he figured it out, Trev didn't care. Dom could keep his secrets. Trev certainly had his own. And Dom was never going to make it work anyway. How would Dom know the first thing about building a Token?

None of them really knew how they worked. You couldn't just wave a dead person's finger around and expect something to magically happen. There were rules and rituals. There was probably a book somewhere with diagrams. Not that they had anything like that.

The Wardens, however, probably had all kinds of stuff locked in a cabinet somewhere. Not for the first time, Trev imagined what it might have been like if he had stayed and learned everything that the Wardens knew. How many mistakes could he and Sam have avoided over the years? But no, that was not an option. Not after what they had done.

When Gregory finally came back, Trev was just about to try a third password. He wasn't sure how many attempts he would get before the phone would lock up. For all he knew Sam had set it to self-destruct or something after a certain number of tries. So far he'd tried "Fuck Off" and "Keep Out." He closed his eyes and tried to picture the magic word floating around inside his sister's head.

"What were you thinking?" Trev murmured, when he heard the front door open.

It was as though they had been two different people back then. Literally—a different Trev and Gregory who stayed up talking late at night. A different Trev who used to run his fingertips over the curves of Gregory's arms and stomach. A different version of Gregory's arms and stomach.

Time had wiped those months clean. Time had built them new bodies with no trace of the other left on their skin.

"Find anything?" Trev asked, because it was easier to be the first one to speak with Gregory. Trev hated silence.

Gregory rubbed his eyes. "The cracks aren't any

bigger. Maybe your sister did something right after all."

Trev flushed. He knew what Gregory thought of Sam—what he had always thought of her. That she was a fuck-up. And how often had Trev thought the exact same thing? How many times had he cursed his sister for her lack of self-control—for how quick she was to jump into something? Literally. He still was sick to his stomach with what was almost certainly an ulcer when he thought about that day at Duck Shit Lake (as he had started to call it in his head).

But it wasn't just that day. Trev could list all the ways that he had almost lost her. New Mexico. Texas. The lake. And now that fucking crack upstairs that had almost devoured her.

Even though Sam thought of herself as some badass "Xena warrior princess" type, the truth was she constantly had to be rescued. He sometimes lay awake at night and remembered how Sam had looked when he fished her out of the lake. That was what she had done to him over the years—turned him into an old man.

He should have stood up for her now, with Gregory, even if Sam wasn't around to hear it. But it was too late. It was too late for so many things. It was even too late to call Sam by her real name, Matilda.

Moss wasn't even their real last name. It was Meyers. Sam had chosen Moss when she sloughed off *Mattie* in favor of Samantha. She would probably have exchanged her skin if there had been a way to do it.

Trevor wouldn't give up his name, but he shortened it. Trev. It felt new. New enough. What Mattie . . . what *Sam* didn't realize was that it didn't matter how far you ran or how many different names you tried on. People could never escape the past.

"So, how do we close the cracks?" Trev asked.

Gregory sat down across from Trev. He didn't meet Trev's eyes, but looked down at his own phone instead. "We don't. Not yet. First, we find your sister and take care of Jackson before he comes back and finishes ripping apart this town."

Take care of . . . that's what they had said when referring to ghosts. But it wasn't the same thing with Jackson. You can't kill a ghost—it's already dead.

Trev thought about the lake again, and how Jackson had probably saved Sam's life. The way Jackson had looked at Sam while she coughed her lungs up on the shore . . . the way she had looked back at him. If Trev found his sister, he was going to break her heart.

He looked down at the phone in his hands again. Then Trev typed in the words, *duck shit.*

"Oh fuck," Trev gasped. He was in.

Sam's search history was about what Trev would have expected. A review of the latest episodes of *The Bachelorette.* A *Game of Thrones* blog. Random searches for different kinds of knives. And then he saw it—ferry times to Seattle.

"So, she's in Seattle," Dom said, looking at Sam's phone over Trev's shoulder. "I mean, we could have just guessed that without looking at her phone. Are there even any other cities around here? But where in Seattle?"

"Or she drove though Seattle on her way to any other fucking place in Washington state," countered Trev. "And would she really risk all of the ghosts in a city? With Jackson?"

Gregory held out his hand, and Trev handed him the phone, even though it made him feel like a fucking lap dog.

"We have to look for her," Gregory said, swiping through Sam's pictures. "And if Seattle is our only lead, then we go to Seattle."

Trev almost snatched the phone back when Gregory got to a picture of the Halloween party. There was Jackson smiling for the camera in his sailor costume. That costume was now a bloody mess in a landfill somewhere.

Gregory swiped to another picture, and Trev saw the red of Macy's cape. The cape was the only part of her in the picture.

Trev had hoped that Dom wouldn't notice the picture, but Dom made a little noise. It was just a quick inhale, but Trev's heart twisted at the sound.

"So, you really think we should just ignore the cracks?" Trev asked. "Just leave them and run off to Seattle where my sister will be as easy to find as a needle in a fucking field of hay?"

"I think we could find her," Dom said. "She doesn't exactly blend in. And she has my car. I could still just report it stolen. What do you think?"

When Gregory didn't answer either of them right away, Trev held out his hand for his sister's phone. Gregory waited a beat too long before returning it.

Gregory sighed. "We're not going to ignore the cracks," he said, finally answering Trev's earlier question. "I've made some calls. We have backup coming."

Trev wasn't surprised that Gregory had called the Wardens. And he shouldn't have felt so disappointed either.

Chapter Thirteen

Trev leaned against the metal railing on the topside of the ferry. It was starting to rust—not just the railing but the whole ferry, in wide, sporadic patches. He'd looked it up, the first time they rode the ferry on their way to Grey Hills. The saltwater did it, ate away at the boat like a cancer.

Cold rain was spitting into his face, but Trev didn't want to be inside. Gregory was in there. The hour drive to the ferry terminal had been way too long. There was so much they should have been discussing—where to look first, what to do if they did find Sam. What to do if they found Jackson and not Sam.

That was the option Trev didn't even want to think about. What was that old saying? If you caught a tiger by the tail, you had better not let it go.

What if Sam had already let go?

But they didn't say more than a few words in the car. He and Gregory had sat in silence while the rain blurred the windshield, and the headlights from the passing cars made Trev's eyes scratchy. Trev ended up having to take out his contacts, which he hated. He always felt exposed when he wore his glasses. He didn't want to be Clark Kent today. He wanted to be Superman.

Sam would have given him such shit for comparing himself to Superman.

Gregory had a new car, or at least new since they left him in Texas. He used to drive an old white Camry, but now he had a gaudy orange Subaru Crosstrek. Riding in it made Trev feel like they were in the *Jurassic Park* movie—the original one. There was something reptilian about the car.

Where did you get the money for this thing? Trev might have asked Gregory, but Trev had a feeling he already knew. The Wardens' pockets ran deep. That was something Trev had known for a long time now. Ever since they wrote Trev and his sister a huge check to pay off their guilt. It was made to look like a life insurance policy, but Trev didn't believe it. His parents weren't the type of people to balance their lives against fifteen million dollars.

It was money to keep them silent, Trev had told his sister once he figured it out. Money so he and Sam would leave and forget about the things their father was working on for the Wardens. Sam didn't believe him. She always said Trev was becoming a conspiracy nut, and that he needed to just move on with his life. Nothing would bring their mother or Jamie back, so they might as well start living.

Trev wondered if his sister realized what a hypocrite she was, thinking that chasing ghosts was the same as *moving on*. But Sam never had much of an imagination. She understood the things she could see and feel and taste. Sam thought she was the one who was living her life, but she seemed to do everything in her power to make that life as short as possible.

For fuck's sake, she just ran off with a ghost like she was smuggling a puppy out of a pet store under her coat.

Trev looked down at the churned-up water. He wondered what his sister would think if he climbed right over this railing and let himself fall into the path of the ferry, where his body would surely be sucked under and shredded by a propeller. How would she like to just watch, helpless, while he disappeared beneath the waves? Because that was exactly what Sam had done when she decided to vanish with Jackson. For all Trev knew, his sister was already dead.

"Hey." Trev felt a hand on his shoulder. He whirled around, his back against the railing. It was Gregory, of course.

"I thought you were gonna lose your glasses,"

Gregory said, smiling a thin smile. "You were lean-ing over so far."

Trev shrugged. He didn't need to do the *small-talk* thing just to make Gregory feel more comfort-able. It wasn't *his* job to put Gregory at ease.

Gregory stepped beside him, gripping the rail. In the distance Trev could see the tall buildings growing bigger and bigger as Seattle seemed to emerge from the sea.

"Listen," Gregory said, "what I told you . . . before you all left Texas. Did you tell your sister?"

Trev almost didn't answer. Then a seagull flew beside them and hovered a few feet away. It turned its little black eyes toward them, probably begging for food. But something about the bird made Trev's chest ache. Maybe it was the arch of its wings and how the air perfectly supported the bird's body. How it must feel to be weightless like that . . .

He shook his head, and said, "No." Trev wasn't sure if Gregory heard him over the wind rushing past, but then he saw Gregory nod.

"Thanks," Gregory said, though Trev could barely hear it. Then Gregory pushed off the railing and went back inside, leaving Trev to watch the city loom closer and closer on the horizon.

When they were almost to the dock, just before Trev went back to the car, he thought he saw something in the water. Among the kelp and the white froth of the waves, Trev thought he saw a face looking up at him.

Fucking ghosts. He'd forgotten how bad cities could be.

Chapter Fourteen

"Okay, where do we start?" Gregory asked. They had parked the car in a garage a few blocks up from the water and had set out on foot. It would be easier, they figured, to spot her if they were walking.

"Just start knocking on hotel doors I suppose." Trev had the hood of his raincoat pulled tight around his face. The raindrops had only gotten bigger and colder until they formed a slushy hybrid of rain and snow.

When they had first driven off the ferry, Trev saw the ghost of a teenage girl staring at him from the sidewalk. She was wearing ripped jeans and a black shirt, and Trev could tell she was a ghost because another pedestrian walked right through her.

The ghost then tried to grab the man who had passed through her ghostly form, but her hands wouldn't latch on. She looked like she was screaming. Trev met her eyes as Gregory drove past. He could practically taste the anger that was coming off her. Bitter oranges and bile.

Now, with a whole city to sift through searching for one redhead, Trev felt a hopelessness begin to creep into the base of his throat. He swallowed down the lump that had formed and blinked his tired eyes up at the tall, blank-faced buildings. Where to start, indeed?

"So," Trev said, wiping his rain-splattered glasses off on his jeans, "maybe we should start with the downtown hotels? We could just show them her picture. Ask if anyone's seen her?"

"What kind of place would she stay?"

"Somewhere nice, probably. With a pool and

those big puffy white bathrobes. She likes to steal those." Trev got out his phone and did a search for hotels in the downtown area. He had already done this search several times on the drive to the ferry and on the ferry itself, but he hadn't written anything down. It was comforting to be able to type something into his phone and have an answer. It almost felt like he was doing something.

Gregory frowned. "But wouldn't she know we'd look for her in a nice hotel? Maybe she's in a motel by the freeway? Or an abandoned house somewhere?"

Trev blinked more rain out of his eyes. "Or she'll think that *we'll* assume that *she'll* avoid the nice hotels and go stay in the fanciest one because she's my sister, and she has very little impulse control." Trev pointed up the block. "There's a Four Seasons that way. Shall we just start knocking?"

The first three hotels they checked were

discouraging to say the least. No one had seen anyone like Sam. Trev had a few decent pictures of her on his phone, but when he said that she also had a black eye and possibly a split lip, all of the front desk people had given him these really weird looks when they said that nobody fitting that description had checked in.

He told them she was his sister and that she was a runaway, which was so close to the truth that Trev felt almost guilty, like he was lying to them about telling a lie. It hurt his head when he thought about it too much.

In the third hotel, which was an old building from the 1800s, Trev and Gregory stopped to have some coffee. Trev just wanted to go across the street to a Starbucks and get his regular Caramel Macchiato, but Gregory wanted to stay in the disgustingly quaint little hotel restaurant.

"You could go to a Starbucks anywhere," Gregory said, looking at him with that wheedling smile he always used when he knew he was going to get his own way.

For a moment, Trev almost forgot where they were and how much time had passed since he last saw that smile. He almost smiled back.

Instead, Trev muttered, "That's why I like Starbucks." But he didn't argue further, and let Gregory find them a table by the window, where they could keep an eye on the people walking by. The odds were so slim that Sam would actually walk past this building, at this exact time, but Trev wouldn't stop scanning the faces. They were all mostly half-hidden beneath hoods or, in a few instances, umbrellas.

"So," Trev began after they ordered their coffees—a caramel latte for Trev and just a boring drip coffee for Gregory—"when is your 'backup' getting here? Are we talking black helicopters and men in shiny sunglasses? Like, total *Men in Black* or something?"

"It's just a few guys. We're not as . . . exten-sive . . . as you seem to think."

"Your *creepy-as-fuck* cult isn't extensive?" Trev said, "Well, I guess that's good news." Two ghosts walked past the window, arm-in-arm. A lady with a long, old-fashioned looking dress and a man in a suit.

Trev nodded towards them, "See them?"

"Yeah." Gregory looked down at his napkin. "I should go deal with them, but we just don't have time right now." From the washed-out look of Gregory's face, and the bags that lingered under his eyes, Trev wondered if the problem was time, or simply that Gregory didn't have enough strength to take care of them.

Destroying ghosts wasn't always easy. It wasn't just a flick of the wrist and they're gone. It took something from you. It always left Trev shaky, hungry, and feeling like he'd just run a marathon—an endless race where there was no end, and all the other runners were dead.

Their coffees arrived and they drank them mostly in silence. Even when they didn't speak, Trev could feel unspoken words rise off the table like the steam from their drinks and hover around their heads.

Gregory: *Why did you leave me?*

Trev: *Why did you come back?*

There was no answer to either question, not really. Not anything either one of them would be satisfied with. And that was exactly why Trev had never wanted to see Gregory again after Gregory had told him the truth about what happened to Trev's dad. It was like that Schrödinger's cat thing again, but not quite. Sometimes two realities can exist at the same time, but not the same place. Two truths that will rip each other apart if they aren't kept locked away in separate parts of the brain.

I love him.

He helped the Wardens kill my family.

Even though Trev looked outside while he drank his latte (not as sweet as Starbucks, but richer), he could see Gregory's reflection in the window. Didn't Gregory know that was exactly where he was supposed to stay?

A ghost in the glass. A memory.

Chapter Fifteen

Sam paid the driver, then she and Claire climbed out of the taxi. They were standing in front of a perfect-looking, blue Craftsman house. Someone had already put up a string of Christmas lights along a row of shrubs, which Sam thought was just going a little too far for early November.

The Queen Anne neighborhood, it turned out, was quaint and peaceful—especially when compared to the noise and bustling of downtown. It kind of reminded Sam of Grey Hills. Queen Anne was even high up on a hill, overlooking Seattle's downtown.

Claire got out an umbrella and unfolded it above their heads. "Where to now?" she asked.

The pattering sound of the rain above their heads was distracting, and Sam had to take a moment to remember the directions. After several near-sleepless nights, Sam was having trouble keeping her brain from just throwing up the white flag and calling it a day.

"Um," Sam began, looking around. "I think it's a few blocks that way." She pointed past the blue Craftsman to where the old, uneven sidewalk drifted up a tree-lined street. As they walked, Sam and Claire had to keep stepping over huge puddles that had filled in cracked and sunken bits of concrete, and places where tree roots had broken through.

Sam knew they were at the right address as soon as she saw it. A large, white house stood before them, with red shutters. It looked exactly like it did on Google Maps, except that it had been sunny whenever those pictures had been taken. The front yard was perfectly manicured with grass that was still green, even in winter.

"He lives here?" Claire asked, scrunching up her nose when Sam nodded. "This place is practically a mansion. I had hoped he'd be taking his exile a bit harder." Then Claire took her phone out of her pocket and glanced at the screen. "We've been gone for almost thirty minutes. We're fine, right? We still have a few more hours?"

"Yeah," Sam said, flicking water off the sleeve of her coat. "We should have enough for . . . well, whatever it takes."

After ringing the doorbell three times, Sam thought that maybe the house was empty. She was about to pull her small lock-picking kit out of a coat pocket when she noticed a little cement path leading to the side of the house.

Following it, she and Claire found another door that looked like it led to a basement. She tried to peer in one of the basement windows, but the curtains were drawn.

"Knock," Sam said to Claire, nodding towards the door. She pulled a pick out of her pocket and held it behind her back. She could have pulled out Macy's knife, but she didn't want to make Claire more nervous than she already was.

Claire shook her head, taking a step back, carrying the umbrella with her. "You knock. What if he doesn't even live here?" Claire reached into her purse, which Sam now knew meant she had her fingers on her pepper spray.

"Wuss," Sam said, stepping up and rapping on the door. They waited a few moments, just listening. Nothing. Sam lifted her hand to knock again when the door cracked open.

"Hello?" a deep voice asked. Vice Principal Fitch was home after all.

Chapter Sixteen

Mr. Fitch looked exactly how Sam remembered him: tall, with thinning hair and the very beginnings of a beer belly. While he had always worn a suit and tie when he was the vice principal at Grey Hills High, today he was wearing an old, faded Seahawks T-shirt and sweats.

"Can I help you?" Mr. Fitch asked them, first peering down at Claire, and then giving Sam and her sunglasses a bewildered look.

"May we come in?" Sam asked in her nicest voice. "We'd like to talk to you about the Grey Hills fire."

"No," Mr. Fitch started to close the door, "Sorry, I'm not doing any more interviews."

Sam half-stepped into the doorway. "This isn't exactly an interview."

Mr. Fitch shook his head. "I told you I have nothing to say. Please leave." But there was something in his eyes. Sam had seen it before, whenever she sat beside those sad, drunk men in bars. Deep down, Mr. Fitch wanted to talk to someone.

"We're coming in," Sam said, pushing forward.

Sam knew it had been a long shot when she asked Trev to track down Mr. Fitch's address a few weeks after the gym fire. Sam had been convinced that the sketchy vice principal knew something about the original Fire. Now she hoped he would know something about the ghost that was controlling Jackson.

Mr. Fitch simply had to know something. It was just too much of a coincidence, the way he had shown up in town right before the school fire, and how he had personally championed the Lock-In to make sure it went on. If Mr. Fitch really was just an ignorant bystander, then Sam was officially out of ideas and that simply wasn't an option.

"No," Mr. Fitch said again, actually trying to shove Sam out of the doorway. "I'll call the police." There was a tinge of panic in his voice.

Then Claire stepped forward. "Hi, Mr. Fitch. Remember me?"

He gave her a blank look.

"No?" Claire continued. "I'm a little insulted. Do you know how long it takes to look this nice? I mean, the time I spend on my hair alone . . . Anyway, here's the deal." She smiled sweetly at Mr. Fitch, batting her long eyelashes. "You let us in and answer my friend's questions, or I tell the police that you molested me when you were working at Grey Hills."

His blank expression changed to one of horror.

"And then you lured us poor country schoolgirls to your house in the big city. Who knows what you might have done to us had I not called the police?"

Mr. Fitch's mouth opened and closed a few times. His face was bright red. Finally, he said in a loud, almost comedic whisper, "Okay, just get inside before someone sees you."

As he led them into the small basement apartment, Mr. Fitch grumbled something that sounded a lot like, *I don't need this*, under his breath.

Claire had been mistaken. Apparently, Mr. Fitch wasn't currently benefitting from all of the legendary Grey riches after all. The neighborhood might have been wealthy, but his small basement apartment was just depressing.

There were old microwave-dinner containers on the counters, and the air smelled like spoiled milk and beer. He had an old TV, one of those boxy ones that absolutely no one had anymore. Sam didn't know if thrift stores would even accept them as donations.

"Alright," he said once they were all sitting in the cramped living room area of the basement, which held a small couch and a rocking chair. "What do you want to know?" In this part of the basement, the air didn't smell as sour. It smelled like incense.

Sam took a seat on the couch, next to Claire, leaving the rocking chair for Mr. Fitch. "We know you were working with Lorna Evans," Sam said. "We know you tried to burn all those kids."

"I would never—"

"Just cut the act," Sam said, not letting him finish. "We know all about it. We know about the ritual, and the Door that you were trying to keep closed. We know that you failed, and when Lorna vanished, you just ran away like the scared chicken shit that you are. That's right, isn't it? You had no idea what would happen when the Door to the Dead opened so you ran as far as you could."

Sam laughed. "Which wasn't actually all that far, was it? Seattle? Now, if I was going to make a run for it, I might try Alaska or maybe Florida. Somewhere in another time zone at least."

Mr. Fitch shifted in his seat, and the rocking

chair gave a creaking groan. "Are you done?" he asked.

"Almost. We know all that. But what we don't know is why. What convinced you to do it? Why try to kill all those people to keep the Door closed? And—"

"And?" he prompted, giving her the same look he might give a spider he wanted to squash. One that he thought might be poisonous.

And how can I save Jackson? "And what else do you know? About your family, I mean. The Greys."

Claire chimed in, "And we'll know if you're lying."

Sam raised an eyebrow at Claire, and she shrugged back. Did Claire think that Sam had superpowers or something? Or was Claire the superhero in this scenario?

"Well," Mr. Fitch said, still creaking his chair back and forth, "it sounds like you know everything, don't you? Where could I even begin, hmm?" His voice was dripping with sarcasm. Sam wanted to punch him in his stupid, unshaven, blotchy face, but she'd probably get some leftover food residue on her fist.

Sam said, "Just start at the beginning. Tell us what you know, and we'll decide what's important."

Mr. Fitch looked at Sam and Claire in disbelief. "Is this really happening? Am I really being interrogated by a pair of fucking high school girls?"

Sam didn't answer, but she also didn't look away. He squirmed in his seat, and then glanced up at the clock on the wall. Silence was a surprisingly good motivator. After almost two minutes of achingly uncomfortable quiet, he began.

Chapter Seventeen

"It's not as though I wanted to hurt all those kids. I'm not a monster." Mr. Fitch was looking down at his hands as he spoke.

A few of his nails, Sam noticed, were bitten down until the skin was red and angry. That's how Sam's fingers had looked the year after her mom and brother died. She tried not to bite them anymore, but sometimes she still found her fingertips tapping at her mouth, or her teeth clicking across her thumbnail.

"*You're* not a monster?" Claire asked. Sam shook her head at Claire—she didn't want them to interrupt Mr. Fitch if he was finally talking.

Claire ignored her completely and went on, "Then what are you, huh? What do you call yourself? A hero? A brave man who listens to children screaming and does nothing? What the fuck do you call someone who does a thing like that?" Claire's body was shaking, almost imperceptivity, but Sam could feel the cushion on the couch vibrating. She put her hand on Claire's arm.

Mr. Fitch stopped rocking his chair and brought a hand up to his lips. He regarded Claire with wide, solemn eyes. He lowered his hand back to the chair and said, softly, "A man like that . . . I suppose that's how I'll be judged. By my worst decision. By my worst day."

He went on, his voice growing louder. "In that case, I'd call a man like that damned. Damned to his own private hell for the things he's done. But yes, to answer your question. Yes, I'd call him brave. Because sometimes things need to be done. Hard choices need to be made, even if no one wants to be the one to make those choices. Even if everyone wants to look the other way. Sometimes things need to be done, and if that man steps up and says, yes—yes, I'll do the unthinkable so that the unimaginable will not come to pass . . . I'd call him very brave." He sounded like he was giving a speech. Sam wondered if Mr. Fitch told himself these words when he was by himself. If he spoke them to a mirror.

The whole time Mr. Fitch was talking, Sam kept her hand on Claire's arm, ready to do something—shake her if necessary—if she said something to stop him. When it was clear that he was finished, Sam leaned forward.

She wanted to get this right.

"Then tell us," Sam said, trying to make her voice as kind as possible. "Just tell us what happened. We can't understand if we don't know. And that's all we want. We don't want to judge you. We don't want to punish you. We just want to know your story. What happened that first week of school? What did you do?"

Claire looked like she wanted to protest, but when Sam narrowed her eyes in warning, Claire kept quiet.

"Will you?" Sam asked when Mr. Fitch was still silent. "Will you please just tell us your story? Help us understand your side of things?"

His hand went to his mouth again, absently tugging on his bottom lip. Mr. Fitch looked hesitant, almost scared—the look a deer might give when it is deciding whether to go on eating or to bolt from a strange sound. Finally, he said, "Okay. If you'll listen. If you'll really listen, I'll talk. I'm not who you think I am. I'm not a man who would murder children."

Sam nodded back in what she hoped was encouragement, then nudged Claire until she nodded, too.

Mr. Fitch nodded as well, as though giving himself permission to speak. "Alright. First you need to know that I'm not like the others. The Greys, I mean—my family. I'm not strong like they were. My mother used to tell me stories about her dad."

"Principal Grey?" Sam asked, even though she already knew the connection. Trev had even found a family tree online, with little branches splitting off to mark the generations. Mr. Fitch had been a tiny, insignificant-looking sprig near the bottom of the page.

"Yes, Richard Grey. He died protecting everyone, did you know that? He died to close the Door. He was a hero."

"How do you know that?" Sam asked, even though she was a little worried about offending him. "How do you know that he was even involved? Maybe your grandpa just burned up along with everyone else and knew nothing about any ritual? It was Lorna, wasn't it? She was behind it?"

Claire gave Sam a very confused look, and she made a mental note to figure out how many holes she, Trev, and Dom had left in Claire's haphazard education from two nights earlier. The poor thing must be so confused. Claire was surprisingly accepting of everything so far. Maybe something was a little wrong with Claire's head for her to believe in ghosts so easily.

Mr. Fitch shook his head. "That's not what happened."

"Then what," Sam said through gritted teeth, "happened?" She was struggling to stay patient.

He narrowed his eyes. "You say you know about ghosts, but can you see them? Can you see a ghost when he is looking out from another person's eyes?"

Sam's heart clenched. Was he talking about Jackson? But then Mr. Fitch continued. "I could see my grandfather when Lorna spoke to me. He was inside her body. She had kept him, well, not alive, but kept him close. Kept him safe all those years. He's the one who spoke to me. He told me what needed to happen."

Claire shifted on the couch, and by the almost

comical frown on her face, Sam could tell that Claire was suppressing a comment or two. Sam squeezed her arm in thanks.

"You're saying that Principal Grey had possessed Lorna?" Sam asked.

"Possession . . . I hadn't thought of it in those terms before. That word sounds rather *Exorcist*, doesn't it? But yes, it was Richard, through Lorna, who told me about the Doors. He told me what would happen if we let the Door open."

"And what, exactly, was that?" Sam asked.

"I don't know," he replied.

"Bullshit," Sam hissed under her breath, and then tried to regain her composure. "I mean, you have to know something. Otherwise what were you doing all this for? Because your dead grandpa told you to do it? I liked my grandparents and all, but if they told me to go burn up my classmates in a fire, I'd probably at least ask them a few questions first. You know, your basic *who* and *why* for starters." The smell of incense was really starting to annoy her. What was up with the incense, anyway? That seemed way too *hippy* for Mr. Fitch.

Mr. Fitch rubbed his face. His fingers made a soft rasping sound against his stubble. Sam almost thought he wasn't going to answer her when he finally said, "Imagine a place where the dead do not die. Where they stay forever. Where they are free to hurt and torture the living, and no one can stop them. That was the world my grandfather wanted to prevent.

"I didn't want those students to die. I wasn't even sure . . . well, I suppose I could figure out what Richard and his pet ghost with the goggles were going to do. And then Lorna . . . did she suffer much?" Mr. Fitch cocked his head at Sam, and said, "How did you stop her? I can only guess at what you did to her in the end. I'm just assuming it was you. I read that she's still missing. Did you bury her too? Along with the body of that poor girl they found in the woods?" He gave Sam a thin smile, and she wanted to rake her nails across his face.

Claire gave a little gasp when he mentioned *that poor girl* but didn't say anything.

"We didn't touch Lorna. Whatever happened to her was of her own making." Sam took hold of Claire's arm again, just in case the girl was going to launch herself at Mr. Fitch for mentioning Macy. Sam hoped Claire could hold it together just a little longer.

This questioning was getting her nowhere. Sam already knew about the Door, and who caused the fire. None of this was helpful. None of this was going to help Jackson.

Sam took a deep breath to steady herself and said, "Does the name Eli Grey mean anything to you?"

"Why?" Mr. Fitch scratched his face again. That was his tell, Sam realized—rubbing his chin. If they were playing poker Sam would have wiped the floor with him. He knew something.

"Because I asked," Sam said, leaning forward in her seat. She looked up at the clock. They still had some time, but it was dwindling. She would have to get back soon or else who knew what Eli might do.

"I've heard Eli's name, but I've heard about dozens of old Greys, who lived and died before I was born. Just old, dead history." He wasn't exactly lying, but he knew something. As a liar herself, Sam knew how to spot them.

Sometimes the best way to unnerve a liar was to tell the truth. Sam took off her glasses so Mr. Fitch could get a good, clear look at her busted-up face, then said. "Eli Grey possessed my friend. Then he tried to kill me."

"He's inside her?" Mr. Fitch asked, pointing at Claire. His voice took on a slightly shrill tone. "And you brought her here?"

"No, asshole," Claire snapped. "This is my own charming personality."

Sam cut in, "A different friend." She tried to

keep her voice steady, but she felt herself getting choked up. "And I think he's dying."

Too much truth, Sam thought, not letting herself start to cry.

"You should have told me," Mr. Fitch said. He leaned over toward a side table and opened a drawer. "You should have told me this the moment I opened the front door."

"Whoa!" Sam said, reaching into her pocket for the knife. "What are you doing?"

Instead of answering, Mr. Fitch pulled out another stick of incense and a lighter. He lit the end of the incense and put it in the jar on the table that already held one stick of incense. As a second thin plume of smoke rose toward the ceiling, Sam's eyes watered from the strong, spicy scent.

"What is that all about?" Claire asked, waving her hand in front of her face to waft away the smell.

"Ghosts hate it," Mr. Fitch said. He was still

gripping the lighter in his rather large fist. "They stay away if you light this special incense."

"That is bullshit," Sam said again, shaking her head. "What are you talking about?"

"It's true. My grandfather told me."

"Your grandfather, the ghost? Um, something isn't really adding up here." Sam coughed. Her throat still ached.

"All I know is that if you have a ghost following you around, I don't want any part of it. In fact, I think you two should leave now. Just go, and don't come back."

Something moved in the shadows behind Mr. Fitch. Sam was just getting ready to get out Macy's little knife and see how persuasive she could be, when she saw someone stand up behind the old vice principal.

The ghost was wearing a bright red cloak, with the hood pulled up over her head. Sam couldn't see her face, but she instantly knew who it was.

If Claire saw Macy too, she gave no indication.

"We're not leaving until you tell us something about Eli Grey," Sam said, trying to keep her eyes on Mr. Fitch's face and not on the dead girl standing behind him.

He shook his head. "I don't know anything. You can tell Eli that. Actually, don't tell him anything about me, okay? You haven't told him where I live, have you?"

Macy raised a hand until it hovered just above Mr. Fitch's balding blonde hair. He shivered, as though sensing her there. If he turned his head, would he be able to see her? She had no idea how powerful Mr. Fitch actually was—how much he could see.

"Tell me about Eli," Sam said again. "Anything. Anything you might have heard."

Shaking his head, Mr. Fitch started to protest again, but then suddenly stopped. Macy had her hand on his scalp. Then her fingers sank into his head. Mr. Fitch shivered once, violently, and his eyes rolled back into his head.

"Shit!" Claire said, standing up. "Is he having a seizure or something? Should I call 911?"

Sam pulled her back down. "Just wait," she said, barely breathing. "Just wait a sec. I want to see what happens."

Macy moved her hand, and Mr. Fitch jerked his arm. Then he started to groan. After almost a minute of sifting through the man's brain, Macy stopped. She seemed to have found what she was looking for. Sam still couldn't see Macy's face, but she imagined that she was smiling.

Ask him, said the voice in the back of Sam's head. Macy's voice. *Ask your questions now.*

When Sam and Claire left his apartment almost thirty minutes later, Mr. Fitch was still in the rocking chair. His head tipped forward, and he was sucking in shallow, uneven breaths. On their way out, Sam took his phone, dialed 911, and left it ringing on the counter. Maybe he didn't deserve it, but *Sam* wasn't a monster.

Chapter Eighteen

"No, we haven't found her," Trev said into the phone. Dom had just called him. Again. Dom had been calling almost every single fucking minute since they left Grey Hills. "Stop calling," Trev said. "I'll call you if we find anything."

It was almost ten p.m., and Trev was standing outside of yet another hotel. He had ducked outside when Dom called because he didn't really want Gregory listening to his conversation. There had been altogether too much Gregory lately.

"Unless you're dead. Then you won't call me," Dom sounded particularly grumpy this time.

Waiting around was not one of Dom's strong suits.

"Maybe I *will* call you if I'm dead," Trev said. "Maybe I'll go haunt a cell phone tower." It was snowing again, and even though Trev was standing beneath an awning, a few flakes drifted onto his arm.

Dom sighed. "Just call me, okay? I've got nothing to do here but worry."

"Jesus Christ. Go take a walk or something. Check on the cracks like you're supposed to be doing. Do some good old-fashioned investigating. *Feet on the street*, and all that." Trev closed his eyes. He and Gregory had been walking all day and he was exhausted. Apparently Trev's most recent routine of blackout drinking and then sleeping until noon was not actually an exercise plan. Who knew?

"When you find Sam, you know what you need to do first, right?"

Trev sighed into the phone. "What?"

"Take my fucking keys away from her."

Trev groaned and then hung up without saying goodbye. All day they had been looking for that goddamned car. They had tromped through every parking garage and down every side street. And the whole day it had kept raining until his jeans and shoes were soaked. When it finally turned to snow about an hour earlier, Trev's chest lightened. He had turned his face up to the sky and wondered that a few degrees in temperature could change his whole mood. Snow was more polite than rain, Trev decided. A gentlemanly precipitation.

Sam probably wasn't even in the city. And if she was, then she would definitely have been smart enough to hide the car where they wouldn't find it. Or if they found it, she would already be long gone. Sometimes it sucked having a twin who was (almost) as smart as you.

Pocketing his phone, Trev went back into the hotel lobby. It was a newer building—all shiny and smelling like paint. Gregory was still waiting in line to talk to someone at the check-in desk.

"Hey," Gregory said as Trev stopped beside him. "So, I was thinking. It's pretty late. Should we just get a room?"

Trev looked down at his feet so Gregory wouldn't see his face flush.

"Two rooms, I meant," he heard Gregory say.

"I know what you meant," Trev said, just as they were waved up to the front desk.

"How can I help you?" a perky brunette asked them.

Gregory flashed her a smile. "Hi, Leslie," he said, like he was already her good friend, and hadn't just read her nametag. "Our friend has already checked in, and I was hoping you could tell us her room number."

"Well," Leslie's mouth turned down at the edges. Even strangers hated to disappoint Gregory. "We really can't give out information about our guests unless . . . " Her smile returned. "Would your friend have listed you on the room?"

Gregory shook his head, and then ducked his head in an *aw shucks* kind of a way that people usually found irresistible. "The thing is, she doesn't know we're here. You see, her brother is a soldier. He just got home from a tour, and she hasn't seen him in almost a year. We want it to be a surprise."

Leslie looked Trev over, probably noting how young he looked. Not to mention short, and weak-looking, and generally un-soldierlike. "Well," she said again. "Um, I suppose I could make an exception. What is her name?"

Gregory's cool smile faltered. "Her name," he said then paused, his dark eyes darting to Trev. He probably just realized that Sam would be staying under a fake name.

Before Gregory could dig himself into a deeper hole, Trev said, "I'm not sure if she gave you her married name or not. She's recently divorced." He took out his phone and showed Leslie a picture of Sam. "You've seen her, right? She probably checked in yesterday?"

Leslie looked at the picture, then licked her vividly white teeth. "I'm sorry. I haven't seen her."

Trev flipped to another picture. In this one Sam was standing beside the yellow house right after they bought it. Her hands were on her hips, like she was a fashion model. "How about now? Are you sure you haven't seen her?" Trev winced at the pleading in his voice.

The woman's eyes darted from the picture on the phone over to the bank of elevators against the far wall. Then Leslie looked back at Trev. "I'm sorry, but I've haven't seen her. And I'm really not supposed to share any guest's information. It's against hotel policy. Now, is there anything else I can help you with . . . ?" Her hands hovered over the keyboard after she asked the last question.

Which wasn't a question at all, Trev realized. It was a dismissal.

"Come on," Trev said to Gregory. "Let's go."

"Yeah," said Gregory, but instead of following Trev out the door, he started walking toward the elevators.

"What are you doing?"

Gregory put his hand on the elevator. "I thought I could feel something." Then he put his cheek against the smooth metal door.

Trev looked over his shoulder. A few of the guests in the lobby were staring. "You're looking pretty freaky right now, just FYI," Trev said. "People are going to think you're molesting the elevator."

"It was just . . . almost a scent. Or a feeling. But maybe I'm just getting tired." Gregory stifled a yawn. At that moment, with his eyes heavy with sleep, and his hair still wet from the snow, Gregory looked fragile. Trev could almost see right through him.

Trev shook his head. No. He wasn't going to do this again. But then he found himself walking back to the check-in counter.

"Hi again," he said to Leslie. "You actually can help me with something. I'd like two rooms."

Trev swore she narrowed her eyes at him, but then she nodded. "I'll just need a credit card to put on file. For incidentals."

As the elevator doors closed in front of them, Trev saw a blond girl walk across the lobby. Something about her clothes, or maybe her build, reminded him of Claire. Trev had been meaning to call and check in with Claire all day, but he kept putting it off. He felt bad for going AWOL right after Macy's body was found. Claire had to be going through hell right now.

Trev took out his phone, but he couldn't bring himself to dial her number. He just didn't have the energy to explain to Claire what was happening. Finally, he texted Dom: *staying at hotel. Can u call Claire?*

A few seconds later he got a text from Dom: *fuck you.*

Chapter Nineteen

Sam had sent Claire to the lobby to get some gummy worms and a bag of peanut M&Ms from the vending machine. Then she bolted the door. She didn't want Claire to see what she was about to do. Sam didn't want to see it herself, but she didn't really have much of a choice. Then she walked over to where Jackson was sleeping on the bed.

She knew he was faking it. Sam could feel the ghost inside him watching her, even though Jackson's eyes were closed.

"You have something you want to say to me?" Sam said, nudging Jackson's arm. He winced and then opened his eyes.

"Yes," he said in a raspy growl of a voice. He probably needed more water. "Why is it that you actually think you're going to win?" He coughed, and Sam wondered, not for the first time, if there was something irreparably broken inside Jackson's body. What would happen if Jackson died? Where would Eli go if he didn't have Jackson's body to hide in anymore?

But was Eli simply *hiding* inside Jackson's body? It seemed more like Eli couldn't leave—that he was trapped inside of Jackson as much as Jackson was trapped with Eli. Otherwise why would Eli stay handcuffed to a bed when he could just float free?

While Macy's hand was inside Mr. Fitch's brain, he had told Sam and Claire a few things about this ghost. Eli was the old principal, Richard Grey's, uncle, and had died in an explosion more than one hundred years earlier. He also had a pesky habit of coming back and possessing people. Eli had possessed Richard's brother, Alexander. Then, after

Alexander hung himself, Eli had moved on to Richard's nephew, Henry Grey.

Henry. If Sam let herself believe Eli, then Henry Grey was the one who killed Macy. Sam thought she knew why. Henry, like his uncle, and been trying to keep the Door to the Dead closed. Macy's death had finished the ritual and closed the Door.

Sam wanted to ask Macy if she was right—if she had figured it out—but Macy didn't just come when she was called. As much as Sam wanted to talk to Macy, she hoped that Macy knew to stay away from the hotel room. Sam couldn't risk a ghost as strong as Macy giving Eli the power he needed to escape.

"Where's the journal?" Sam asked, completely ignoring Eli's melodramatic question.

All this time, Sam had been ignoring the obvious. The journal. It had gone missing right before Jackson showed up on her doorstep ready to kill her. Dom had been right all along—Jackson must have taken it. Or rather, Eli must have *made* Jackson take it.

When Macy's hands were in Mr. Fitch's head up to her wrists, the man had given Sam one particularly useful piece of information. Mr. Fitch might not have even known he said it. At that point, who knew what Mr. Fitch was thinking, or if he even *could* think. But Sam refused to feel guilty for the way she and Claire had left that man, not after he had tried to kill hundreds of people. Hundreds of children!

What Mr. Fitch had whispered (in a disturbingly flat, emotionless voice) was that Eli's journal was a Token.

Mr. Fitch had said that there was a family legend that Eli had made himself a Token while he was still alive. Something to bind him to the earth after he died. Something that would make him powerful. That was when Sam remembered the journal, and how none of the writing had made any sense.

It was just the ramblings of a mad man, they

had thought. But that handwriting—the color. It had looked so faded . . . almost rust-colored. And that was when she realized what she must have been seeing on every page. Blood. Had Eli written the journal with his own blood? Had he woven his hair into the pages? What about bone? How had he worked a piece of his own bone into the journal? Sam wasn't sure she really wanted to know.

If they had Eli's Token, then maybe they could stop him. Maybe they could force him to leave Jackson's body.

Now, in the hotel room, Sam sat down on the bed, next to Jackson's chest. She pulled out Macy's sharp little knife and held it in front of his face.

Jackson raised his eyebrows. He smiled. "Is that some kind of a threat? You expect me to believe that you're going to hurt this boy? With your tiny knife?"

"Where is the journal," Sam asked again. "You

hid it somewhere earlier—before Gregory stopped you. Tell me where it is."

Jackson laughed, but it wasn't his laugh. It sounded like something fragile cracking. "Go ahead," Eli said. "Carve your name into his skin for all I care."

Sam asked one more time. "Where is the journal?" When he didn't answer, she rolled up her sleeve and drew the blade of the knife across her own arm.

Blood welled up from the shallow cut. Jackson flinched and looked away. Sam smiled, and then reached out and forced his head back towards her. She made Jackson look at what she'd done.

"Do you see this?" she asked, holding her bleeding arm right in front of Jackson's face. "See what you're making me do?"

"I could drink your blood," the ghost inside Jackson hissed.

Sam held up the knife again and slowly cut another, deeper line parallel to the first. She had chosen the arm that was scarred from the ghosts in New Mexico, because what the hell, it was already hideous. This hurt worse than it had when the ghosts had cut her, probably because the ghosts had taken her by surprise and she wasn't expecting the pain.

This time, however, Sam knew exactly what she was doing. It was terrible. Her hand shook when she made the second cut, and she felt like someone else was moving it forward. She couldn't possibly be doing this to her own body . . .

She was afraid she had imagined Jackson's reaction to the first cut, but as she carved the second line into her skin, she was certain she saw something flicker across her Jackson's face.

"You're in there, Jackson," Sam whispered. "I know you're in there. I know you can fight him." Then louder, she said, "Or should I start cutting things off? Maybe something small. An earlobe? I don't even know what they're for. What purpose could this hunk of flesh possibly have, in the grand scheme of evolution?" Sam held the blade up to her ear. "Or should I just take the whole thing off? Pull a Picasso?"

"Fuck your ear," said Eli with Jackson's mouth, but Jackson was shaking his head *no*. She couldn't be imagining it. Eli had to have been lying before. Jackson wasn't gone. Not completely.

With her hand shaking even more, Sam pressed down with the blade on the top of her ear. Blood ran down her cheek and the side of her neck. She kept her eyes locked on Jackson's.

Don't make me do it, she pleaded with him with her eyes. *Make me stop.* She whimpered, trying not to scream at the pain. Tears filled her eyes. If she pressed any harder she might lose the ear. *Don't make me do it.*

Then Jackson whispered, "Stop."

Sam paused, still keeping the knife poised above her ear. "Jackson?" she said softly. "Can you hear me?"

Jackson's whole body was shaking, and tears

were spilling down his cheek. "He's so strong," Jackson breathed, then he closed his eyes tight. "My head . . . something's wrong in my head. I can't do this."

"Jackson," Sam lowered the knife and took his hand. "I know. I know how much it hurts. And you don't have to fight for much longer. Just try to remember. Please. Where did Eli hide the journal? Where is it? You need to tell me, and then . . . "

Sam paused, the words catching in her throat. "And then you can let go again. You don't need to hurt anymore. I'll do it. I'll fight him for you."

Jackson nodded, still shaking, still keeping his eyes shut tight. "I remember, but . . . " he gasped, and pulled his handcuffed arms away from the bed. Trying, Sam realized, to clutch his head. He moaned, and Sam could hardly see through her own tears. Her breaths came in deep, gasping sobs, and she tried to get herself under control.

She had to be strong. She had to be in control for Jackson.

"Where is it? Think," Sam said again, pressing her hand to Jackson's sallow, sunken cheek.

In the background, Sam could hear Claire knocking. She hoped the door was thick enough so Claire couldn't hear what was happening.

"The cemetery. I . . . Eli dug up Mabel's bones. The journal's with Mabel." Then Jackson screamed, shaking his head from side to side. Sam covered his mouth, hoping she wouldn't smother him. But she had no idea what she would do if someone heard him. With any luck they would think it was just the TV. But who was Mabel? She remembered the last entry of the journal: *Dearest Mabel . . .*

Sam wanted to ask more questions, but blood was coming out of Jackson's nose. He looked like he was dying.

"Let go, Jackson," she wept. "You can let go now. I'll take it from here." She could find a *Mabel*.

How many dead Mabel's could there possibly be in Grey Hills?

And then Jackson . . . no, Eli . . . sunk his teeth into Sam's pointer finger. She gasped and ripped her hand back. Deep crescents welled with blood. Sam slapped Jackson's face before she could stop herself. He laughed, his teeth covered with her blood.

"Did you enjoy that?" Eli asked, blood dripping down his chin. "That was the last of him, I hope you realize that. That was the last bit of Jackson and you used it up. I hope it was worth it. You'll never see your love again." Then Eli turned his head and spat blood onto the already stained pillowcase.

Sam went to the door and opened it, not even bothering to clean up her arm or the blood from her neck. "I know how to stop him," Sam said breathlessly.

Claire's mouth dropped open. "What happened? What did you do?"

Sam just held out her hand. "I need your phone."

Dom answered on the third ring. "Claire? Did Trev tell you to call me?"

Sam almost couldn't speak. She sank down to the ground, her back against the closed door. Finally, she managed, "The journal. I know where it is." She had called Dom because she was afraid that if she spoke to her brother, she would tell him exactly where she was. She had a sinking feeling that Gregory would still convince the others to kill Jackson and not wait and see if the journal would make a difference.

"Sam? Are you okay?" Dom said, "Is Jackson . . . ?"

Sam covered her mouth, her shoulders shaking. Then she looked up at Claire and made herself take a deep breath. "I'm fine," she said into the phone. She told Dom where to find the journal, and why it was so important. "I need it," Sam said. "I can use it to save him."

"Where are you?" Dom pleaded.

"I'll tell you when you have the journal. When we can stop him. When you have the journal in your hands call Claire's phone." Then she hung up.

Sam set the phone on the ground and wrapped her arms around her knees. Her arm stung, but she didn't care. She hung her head and sobbed.

Then Claire was pulling at her arm. "Let me see it," she said. Sam opened her eyes. Claire pressed one of the hotel's bleached-white hand towels to Sam's cuts, then sat down beside her. They sat in silence for a few minutes, both watching Sam's blood soak up through the towel. Then Claire said, "So, do you want your M&Ms or what?"

Sam laughed despite herself. "Yeah. Yeah, I really do."

Just then the telephone rang. Not Claire's, but the room phone.

Claire started to get up but Sam shook her head. "I'd better get it, just in case." Sam didn't think anyone would care if there was another person in the room, but she didn't want anyone to actually come up to look.

The phone was on the nightstand between the beds. Eli raised his eyebrows at her when she picked it up.

"This is Cassandra," Sam answered, giving Eli a warning look. *Don't make a fucking sound.*

"Oh, hi Cassandra, Leslie here. From the front desk?" Did she think Sam was going to confuse her with another Leslie? "I didn't wake you, did I?"

"Nope," Sam said, still pressing a towel to her bleeding ear. "Wide awake. What's up?" Would twenty-something Cassandra Nelson have said, *What's up?* Would anyone besides Bugs Bunny say that?

"Well, it's probably nothing, but I just wanted to let you know that two gentlemen were asking about you just a few minutes ago. And then they checked into the hotel."

Fuck me. "Oh? Can you tell me their names?"

"Sorry, I'm not supposed to give out guest information, but . . . well, one of them said he was your brother."

"Just two? Not three guys?" Sam asked, and then realized how suspicious that probably sounded. Like she was being trailed by the mob or something.

"I only saw two. The one who claimed to be your brother did look a bit like you—light skin, reddish hair. The other was taller, with dark hair. Do you know them?"

Sam closed her eyes, trying to *feel* her brother in the hotel. Twins should be able to do that. Her body should be able to sense his blood and bones as he walked through the lobby or rode an elevator. She should have already known he was here. Sam hadn't realized it before, but she didn't think that she and Trev had ever spent more than a day apart in the past. Had she even spent a night under a separate roof before? It was pathetic, but she wasn't sure.

"No," Sam answered the woman. "They don't ring a bell."

Chapter Twenty

Trev and Gregory had separate rooms, but Leslie had put them next door to each other. After they got off the elevator on the tenth floor, Trev went straight to his room, unlocked the door with a quick swipe of his card, and went inside.

As he shut the door behind him, his phone buzzed. Trev had a text from Gregory: *goodnight.*

Trev hit reply and then just stared at the blinking curser on his phone. He rubbed his eyes, and then typed: *goodnight.* Just before he hit the send button, Trev deleted *good.* Now it was at least accurate.

Trev took a shower and then lay down on the bed in his boxers because he hadn't remembered to bring any pajamas. The room was so quiet that Trev's ears started to ring. He wanted to sleep. He wanted to close his eyes and let the world disappear for a few hours.

He wanted a drink.

His phone buzzed. "Fucking Dom," Trev muttered, but when he looked it was another text from Gregory. *Not tired*, it said.

Trev had decided to ignore it when his phone buzzed again. This time, Gregory had texted: *hungry*

Trev smiled, then wrote back: *go 2 sleep*

Hungry. I'll eat my pillow.

good 4 u. has fiber

Stop it, Trev told himself, setting the phone face down on the bed. But when his phone buzzed again, he picked it up and turned on the screen.

bored

Trev didn't write back this time. He just stared at the screen until a new message appeared.

??

Again, Trev didn't write back. When there wasn't another text, Trev felt something that should have been relief, but was more like the sensation you get when you're going up in an elevator. Like his stomach was too heavy.

Trev was about turn off the little light by the bed when he heard a knock at the door. It was so soft that for a moment Trev wasn't sure if it really was a knock, or if it was his own heart beating in his chest.

Then there was another knock, louder this time. "Trev?" he heard through the door. "Are you awake?"

"No," Trev called back. A smile he had not asked for spread across his lips. "I'm in the middle of a very important REM cycle."

"I'm starving," Gregory said, his voice still

muffled by the door between them. "I'm never going to sleep if I don't get something to eat."

"They have room service, you know."

Gregory didn't say anything for long enough that Trev wasn't sure if he was still there. Then Trev heard a small voice say, "Can we pretend that you don't hate me? Just for tonight?"

Trev sighed, then got out of bed. He picked up his jeans from their rumpled pile on the floor and pulled them on. Then he walked over and opened the door.

The light in the hall was too bright. Trev almost covered his eyes with his hand. "I don't hate you," he whispered. "I just hate what you did."

"I didn't do anything, Trev."

"You lied."

Gregory shook his head, his hair falling into his eyes. "As far as I can tell, the only thing I ever did to hurt you was tell the truth."

The truth. Those words were too simple.

The truth was that Gregory knew exactly who

Trev and Sam were when he found them in Texas. Gregory had been sent by the Wardens. The same people who had experimented on their dad. The same people who let a ghost get inside his dad's head. If it wasn't for them, Trev's family would still be together, instead of in two side-by-side graves and a jail cell.

Gregory's people had destroyed Trev's family.

And Gregory knew all of this, the entire time they were together. He was a fucking spy.

Another truth—one that Trev didn't want to admit to himself—was that he was tired. Not just physically tired. Trev was tired of the distance between him and Gregory. He was tired of all the months he had spent wanting to pick up the phone and call Gregory just to hear his voice. Of all of the hours he had spent waiting for his own phone to ring.

Trev was so fucking tired of knowing that the only guy he had ever loved had been a lie. That

Gregory had never existed at all—not really. He was just a stranger.

"What do you want?" Trev asked him, still standing in the doorway. Half in and half out. "Why are you here?"

Gregory leaned forward, placing one hand on the door frame. He smiled. "I just want some dinner."

They found one of those twenty-four-hour diners that smelled like a mix of syrup and hamburger grease. Trev ordered a chocolate milkshake and fries, while Gregory ordered a steak—rare. When he sliced into it, the meat oozed a reddish, watery liquid.

"Iron—good for the blood," Gregory grinned.

"You're probably going to get some weird Seattle version of mad cow disease, where the cows are over-caffeinated and tech-savvy," Trev said.

"Wow, topical." Gregory rolled his eyes. "Are you going to start talking about how it rains in Seattle, too?"

"I'm left to wonder, once again, why I don't have my own reality TV show." Trev dipped three fries into his milkshake, and then shoved them all into his mouth. His phone rang. It was Dom. "Stop calling every five seconds," Trev muttered, sending Dom to voicemail. *Timeout*, he thought, putting his phone on silent and sticking it back in his pocket. *I just need a fucking timeout.*

Gregory wrinkled his nose at Trev's food. "I forgot you do that."

"Do what?" Trev asked, not breaking eye contact with Gregory as he systematically stuck seven fries into his milkshake, so the top of his drink resembled a pincushion. "I'm just eating my dinner."

"First of all, you are straight up desecrating those fries. Secondly, since when did a milkshake ever count as dinner?"

"Um, since my mom died, and I had to start cooking my own dinners?" Trev shut his mouth so quickly that he almost bit his tongue. He hadn't meant to say that. He had silently agreed to pretend, just for a few hours, that everything was normal between them. And now Trev had completely fucked that up.

Gregory looked down at his steak. His face started to turn sort of red and blotchy, like his skin couldn't quite decide if it should blush. "I . . . " he began, then trailed off.

Trev sighed, then started sticking his fries in his shake again—submerging each one completely until the chocolate threatened to spill over the rim. "I'm sorry. I didn't mean to say that out loud."

"But you were thinking it."

"Of course I was thinking it. I'm always thinking about it, Gregory. Every day. Every single fucking day I see them there on the kitchen floor. Did you know that there was even blood on the ceiling? I felt something drip onto my head and I looked up and it was blood. Do you think there is a single day that I don't remember how it felt to have my mother's blood fall on me?"

"I know . . . "

"No, you don't know. You will never know what that was like. The only person who *does* know—who could possibly know—has been swallowed up by this city. And instead of looking for her, I'm drinking a fucking milkshake with one of the people who destroyed our lives."

Gregory shook his head, then started to cut up his steak into smaller and smaller pieces. Eventually he said, "I didn't destroy shit, Trev. And you know what? All of that was three years ago. I was only fifteen, too. Same age as you. I didn't know what they were doing."

"But you know now, and you're still with them."

Gregory threw up his hands. "And who else am I supposed to be with? Who else in this country can see what we see or do what we do? I didn't have a sister. I didn't have someone like Dom. The Wardens were the only family I had. They took me in when I had literally no one else. And they aren't *bad*, Trev. They didn't mean to hurt your family. They're trying to save the world."

Gregory had never talked about his family—any parents or siblings. Trev sure as hell hadn't wanted to talk about his own family, so the subject had never come up when they were together. They had mainly talked about what was happening *now*: the ghosts they were hunting, where they should go next. What city or what state. Trev used to imagine traveling the whole world with Gregory, but all they had seen together was Texas. And now, he supposed, Seattle.

Gregory had loved to look at their "Map of the Dead," as Dom always called it, and try to figure out if there was a method to the Doors. Gregory and Dom thought there was a pattern, but Sam didn't. She thought the Doors were random forces of nature, like earthquakes. Trev wasn't sure about the Doors, but he knew that even earthquakes weren't completely random. There was always something that happened—a fault line that slipped.

So, sure, Trev thought there could be a reason behind the Doors, but the thing was, he didn't particularly care. He also didn't care why the sky was blue, or why he could drink three glasses of whiskey without being sick but that fourth one always bit him on the ass.

Things just happened. That's how he felt about the Doors. They existed. He didn't need to know their mother's maiden name or fucking social security number. He didn't need to pick everything apart when it didn't even matter in the end.

The dead didn't come back to life—that was the only truth Trev needed to know.

Trev hadn't said anything for a while—maybe a full minute—and neither had Gregory. Then

Trev looked up from his milkshake. He said softly, "Was it worth it? Did you find out what the Wardens needed to know about me and Sam?" Trev never had understood the Wardens' fascination with them—why they had bothered giving them all that money and then sent Gregory to check up on them. Sure, he and Sam could see ghosts, but they weren't particularly powerful. Trev still had a hard time taking out a ghost without using a knife.

Gregory rolled his eyes. "You still think it was all about you, don't you? You still think you and Sam are the center of the fucking universe."

"Um, that is just a given. But, yeah, I mean, why wouldn't it be all about us? You came to Texas to spy on us—to report back to the Wardens, right? Why else would you be there?"

Gregory looked Trev. "I wasn't there for you, okay? It was Dom."

"What?"

Gregory looked down at his food—pushing the bloody steak around on his plate. "They want Dominick Vega. It's always been him."

Chapter Twenty-one

Trev didn't remember to check his phone again until after they left the restaurant. Three missed calls from Dom.

He tried calling Dom back, but it went to voicemail. *Fuck.* Trev should have answered—it had been a dick move to not answer—but he knew Dom would just call back in a few minutes anyway. He'd been calling all fucking day. And it must not have been important if Dom didn't even leave a message.

When Trev and Gregory were almost back to the hotel, a group of about four or five ghosts surrounded them. One moment the sidewalk was empty, and the next, there were hands reaching out and faces inches away from their own.

One of the ghosts took a swipe at Trev with an open hand. It passed right through his stomach.

"Shit!" Trev hissed as his breath was knocked out of him. He shivered with his whole body and backed away. Where the ghost touched him, his skin tingled.

It was hard to see the ghosts individually. They were just a blur of hazy motion and darkness—it was as though they were made from shadows. He could barely see them, but he couldn't really see past them either.

He couldn't see Gregory.

Another set of fingers raked across Trev's face. It didn't hurt exactly, but lines of tingling numbness spread along his cheek and nose.

He stumbled forward, swatting at the air in front of his face, as though he had been enveloped by a swarm of mosquitoes or flies rather than ghosts. In a few seconds, he was free of them. Trev glanced back and saw that Gregory was still surrounded by the ghosts. They moved around Gregory's body like scraps of dark, gauzy fabric, obscuring his face.

Trev concentrated on each scrap, trying to hold on to just one. His mind caught one of the ghosts, and with an effort that felt like lifting a large rock, Trev took care of it. One down.

He scrunched up his nose—the tingling numbness on his face was starting to wear off. Trev had time to wonder what a regular pedestrian who *couldn't* see ghosts would think about this strange, possibly harmless assault when he heard screaming.

At first, Trev thought it was Gregory, and that the ghosts were actually hurting him. But then Trev realized it wasn't one scream. What he was hearing was many screams, all at once. When he looked closer, Trev saw that Gregory's arms were raised within the mass of ghosts. He could see a few of the ghosts' faces—they were twisted in pain or terror and their mouths were wide open. They were the ones screaming.

Then it was over. The ghosts were gone. Gregory gave Trev a grim smile. "Cities, huh?"

Trev sort of shrugged. He couldn't stop staring at Gregory. For just a moment, right after the ghost vanished, Trev thought he saw a soft, faint light surrounding Gregory's arms and head. He blinked, and the light was gone.

As they walked through the lobby toward the elevators, the woman at the check-in desk—Leslie—gave them a really weird look. The same look she had given them before when they first showed her Sam's picture. Like she had a secret.

"Sam's in this fucking hotel," Trev whispered to Gregory when they stepped onto the elevator. "I just know it. That woman is covering for her." His face flushed, and he was somewhere between smiling like an idiot and feeling sick to his stomach. What would they actually find when they found Sam?

Gregory punched the button for the tenth floor. "You might be right. That explains the death glares from *Leslie*. Sam must have told her we kick puppies or something."

"Okay, so how do we find out what room she's in? The front desk won't tell us, and we can't just knock on all the doors. There's, like, thirty floors."

"We could go back down and hang out in the lobby," Gregory suggested. "Maybe we'll see her come out?"

They stepped out of the elevator on their floor and walked down the hall toward their rooms. The last thing Trev wanted was to sit up all night in the lobby instead of sleeping in the nice, soft hotel bed. Especially after fighting that weird pack of ghosts, Trev's whole body was bone tired.

As they walked past the other doors, Trev noticed that one or two of them had Do Not Disturb signs stuck on the handle. Something about the signs made a little signal flair fire up in the back of his mind. He went back and looked at the sign. Gregory raised his eyebrows, but didn't say anything.

There was nothing special about the signs— every hotel had them. Why was he so sure they were important? *Do Not Disturb*...

When he finally figured it out, Trev felt so stupid for not thinking of it before. Housekeeping. When you stayed in a hotel, someone came in and cleaned your room every single day. Unless you put a Do Not Disturb sign out. If Sam was really in this hotel, she'd have that sign out every single fucking day unless she wanted housekeeping to walk in and find Jackson tied to a chair or locked in the bathroom or wherever she was keeping him.

Trev explained it to Gregory, and he grinned. "Trevor Moss, you are a genius."

"And handsome," Trev said, leaning against the wall. "And possessing a certain touch of *je ne sais quoi*."

"And so humble . . . " Gregory said, taking a step closer.

Trev froze. His first instinct was to take a step back, but with his back against the wall there was no more *back* to go. Slowly, Gregory reached out a hand and touched Trev's cheek. "I missed you," he whispered.

There was something strange about Gregory's eyes. Trev had noticed there was something different about them back in Grey Hills, but this was a million times more extreme. They weren't even Gregory's eyes anymore. They flashed blue, then hazel, then green.

"What's wrong with you?" Trev said. He couldn't move. He could barely breathe.

Gregory backed away like Trev had slapped him. "Nothing," he muttered. "Let's just go find her."

They started on the top floor because Trev said that Sam always liked to be up high. "She's like a cat." It turned out that they couldn't actually go to the very top without a special code, so they started on the next one down—the thirty-third floor.

Trev wanted them to split up and just start knocking on every door with a Do Not Disturb sign, but Gregory wanted them to stick together. "We might need each other," he said, "if we actually find her."

He nodded to Gregory, then rapped on the first door with a Do Not Disturb sign. Trev wondered how many doors they would be able to knock

on—and how many guests they would wake up—
before somebody called security on them.

He knocked again, and the door cracked open.

It was Sam.

Chapter Twenty-two

Dominick Vega lifted his shovel and stabbed it into the cold, muddy dirt of the grave.

He was already completely soaked through from the slushy snow and more tired than he had any right to be from the mile-and-a-half walk to the Hilltop Cemetery. And why, some curious bystander might ask, did Dom have to walk that entire way, carrying a fucking shovel like he was Igor from *Frankenstein*? Well, that would be because Samantha "Selfish Crazy Bitch" Moss had stolen his car.

When Dom had arrived at the cemetery gate, Dom was convinced that it was going to be locked.

He sized up the pointy metal fence, trying to decide if he would be able to boost himself over.

Jackson would have had no trouble, Dom realized. That gangly bastard could have probably just hopped it. And who knows, maybe Jackson had used his new ghostly powers to simply float himself over the top like Magneto from the *X-Men* movies.

Dom hesitantly pushed on the gates, almost expecting to get an electric shock. They opened with a shaky *creak*.

Okay, so no leaping fences required. Which was really for the best because Dom's shoulder, which still hadn't recovered from the gunshot wound, was not going to allow anything that resembled climbing, leaping, or even reaching very far above his own head. Even just getting down a box of cereal from the kitchen cupboard was a stretch. No pun intended.

The cemetery was old, no, *ancient*. Dom wished he had come here in the daylight, when he could have actually seen the crumbling headstones more clearly. While it wasn't completely neglected, the graveyard certainly felt forgotten. There was no discernible path through the graves, just a tangle of tall, dead grass and weeds. Dom found himself almost tripping over headstones while he searched, shining his flashlight to try to find a particular name.

Mabel. That name from Eli's journal. It still sounded so familiar, but he couldn't quite place it. Mabel wasn't exactly a common name, at least not anymore. Hopefully, it wasn't all that common back whenever this Mabel had died.

Dom didn't even know if he'd find her grave here. Jackson hadn't actually told Sam where Mabel was buried. Just that Eli had hidden the journal with her bones—a journal that was also a Token. A Token that, fingers crossed, would let them rip Eli out of Jackson's body.

There were several old cemeteries in Grey Hills. This one just happened to be the closest to the yellow house (Dom had Googled it before he left). Two nights before, Jackson had walked from wherever he had dug up Mabel's grave to the yellow house. That was just before Jackson threw Dom against the wall with his fucking mind and almost killed Sam.

They must have been lovers. Dom remembered the words Eli had written to the girl at the end of his journal: *Death is not the end. I am still here.*

Had Eli known he would become a ghost, even before he died? How could a person possibly know that? How could Eli have been so sure that he wasn't just going to fade into nothingness as soon as his heart stopped beating? Even after seeing and destroying nearly countless ghosts, Dom still didn't know that. He had no idea if death wasn't just the final, slamming door on your way out.

Dom wished he knew what Macy had been thinking in her final moments. Had she been afraid? Did she believe that she'd come back? Had she even had time to think of anything beyond the knife at her throat?

Dom didn't expect to see any ghosts in the cemetery. Ghosts never seemed to just hang out over their graves and moan or rattle their chains like in movies. Ghosts, Dom had found over the years, tended to gravitate instead toward things they remembered while they were alive. Houses. People they had loved.

People they had hated . . .

It turned out to be a fairly small cemetery with only about six or seven rows of headstones. He had already covered most of it in the first five minutes and was about to take another lap when he noticed a patch of dirt near a large poplar tree. Dom smelled it before he saw it—the rich, almost metallic scent of wet, turned-up earth.

It was clear that someone had dug this spot up recently. The earth was darker than the weed-covered plots around it and looked like a freshly tilled garden. He was reminded of a nursery rhyme: *Mary, Mary, quite contrary, how does your garden grow?*

Except this was a garden of bones.

The smell brought him back to when he was young and used to watch his mom plant flowers in the garden she had made of their small San Francisco backyard. She would break apart the packed, loamy dirt around the plant's roots before placing it into the little hole in the ground.

Dom didn't like to think about his parents. He liked to just pretend he had sprung fully formed into his room at the boarding school where they had abandoned him. Did his parents ever even wonder where he had ended up after he ran away from that school? Did they wonder if he was dead?

After shuffling his feet through the surrounding grass, Dom found the fallen headstone. Actually, he tripped over it. When it was new, the marker had probably been quite plain. Now, it was nearly illegible, so he could only just make out the first name: Mabel. The letters had faded as the stone itself was worn away by the wind and the rain. The *M* was the clearest of the letters, so when Dom first tried to read the name he thought it said, *Macy.*

But no . . . Macy didn't have a headstone. She wasn't even buried anymore. Her body was probably on a cold, metal sheet in a morgue.

What would they think of her missing finger? Probably that some sicko had cut it off as a trophy—something out of a movie, like *The Silence of the Lambs.*

His shoulder ached with every shovelful of dirt. Dom's gunshot wound had hurt for so long now that he couldn't really remember what it was like to not be in pain. He had heard of phantom limbs before—where you lose an arm or a leg and you can still feel it there, like it's still attached. The phantom limb sometimes hurt. Or it just itched, and there was no way to scratch it.

Dom's wound was like the opposite of that. He still had his shoulder, but it didn't feel like his shoulder anymore. It was like a rusty joint on an old machine, not a part of his body. There was never a moment that he wasn't aware of the pain, buried deep in his muscle and bone. The pain wasn't *him*, but it was a part of him now. Only the pills he took could start to touch it, but the pills themselves made Dom less himself too. Foggier. Slower.

At least when he took two or three of the pills at once, he'd stop seeing Macy's face every time he closed his eyes.

The grave was deeper than Dom had imagined it would be. Did they really need to bury people the full six feet? That was taller than Dom, for fuck's sake. What if he dug himself so deep that he couldn't get out?

The snow turned entirely to rain when he was about three feet deep. His shoes were completely full of muddy dirt, and he was so thirsty he started just lifting his face to the rain and holding his mouth open. Every now and again, Dom would stop and think to himself, *Why the hell am I out here in the middle of the night digging up a grave?* What were Trev and Gregory even doing right now?

Dom had tried to call Trev a few times right after Sam called him on Claire's phone, but Trev didn't answer his fucking phone. He hadn't left Trev any voicemails, because Trev never took the time to listen to them anyway—he would just call Dom back and he'd have to repeat the whole message.

Now Dom knew that not leaving a voicemail had been unbelievably stupid. It turned out that there was no service in the cemetery. Dom didn't know if his cell carrier was the problem, but there were huge pockets throughout Grey Hills, dead areas where his phone had no signal.

When he was four feet down, Dom thought he heard a noise from somewhere above him, out of the grave. A rustling sound. He paused, mid-shovelful, and listened.

All he heard was the rain, and then a slow, swelling rush of the wind moving the poplar leaves.

Dom leaned back on the shovel and stabbed the earth again. This time he hit something hard. It was the coffin. He knelt down and ran his hand over a wooden surface, trying to feel for the edge. The lid of the coffin felt rough and a bit spongy. Dom's stomach lurched at the thought of what was inside. There was a deep gouge in the wood from the shovel, which made him feel pretty shitty. The poor woman was dead, and now he'd messed up her grave.

Scraping away the dirt from the top of the coffin took a lot longer than he thought because clumps of dirt from the wall kept crumbling back down into the hole. When most of the dirt was cleared away, Dom did his best to step off of the coffin, sinking his feet into the dirt wall. Then he lifted the lid.

He held his breath and pointed his flashlight down into the grave. The first thing he thought as he looked at Mabel's body was, *Why didn't I bring gloves?*

Her bones weren't as gruesome as he thought they might be. He didn't know exactly when she had been buried. Who knew if there was even such a thing as embalming back then, and the wooden coffin probably leaked.

Mabel's arms were folded across her chest, and her head was slightly cocked to one side. From where Dom was standing, it almost seemed like she was looking right at him. Dom had never seen a skeleton before, and it wasn't exactly like he'd expected. In the movies, skeletons seemed to be perfectly white and clean. Her bones were mostly covered by rotting fabric, but where they were exposed, the bones looked darker than he had imagined. Instead of being white, they were more like the color of sand.

When he looked closer at her skull, he realized

that part of it was missing. A large chunk of bone on the side of her head was gone. After shining the light at poor, departed Mabel's face for a few more seconds, Dom averted the beam. He knew it silly, but he felt he was being rude—like she was sleeping and he was going to wake her up.

Where was the journal? Dom assumed it would just be sitting on top of her bones—that Jackson might have tucked the book carefully into Mabel's arms. He shined his light up and down the skeleton, but it was hard to focus his eyes on any one part of her.

The whole time something was nagging at him. *Mabel.* He had heard that name before, hadn't he? And her skull—the way part of it was just gone. It was so familiar. He was still scanning her coffin for the journal that didn't seem to be there when it finally dawned on him.

Mabel Donati. The ghost in the movie theater. After Dom showed Macy the ghost on their "date" to the movies, Macy had done some research about the ghost. Later, after the Lock-In fire, Macy told Dom the ghost's name, and how she had died. Mabel had committed suicide by shooting herself in the head.

Whoever had prepared her body for burial must have tried to put her head back together. When Dom looked closely he could see little cracks around parts of her skull, but a big chunk of bone was still missing.

Dom wondered if microscopic bits of Mabel's head were still in the movie theater. Pieces imbedded in the wall or ground into the floor. Specs of bone so small you'd never even know they were there. Dom had never gone back to take care of Mabel's ghost. He had completely forgotten about her.

He kept looking for the journal in the coffin, but the rain was making everything muddy and slippery, and after a few minutes he knew that Sam had been wrong. The journal just wasn't here.

Dom thought about the exact words Sam had told him over the phone: *Eli dug up Mabel's grave. The journal is with Mabel.*

Oh my God. Dom almost dropped the flashlight. What if Eli didn't actually hide the journal in the *grave*. What if he dug up the bones for some other purpose.

The journal is with Mabel.

Dom needed to call Claire's phone. He thought he knew where the journal was. It wasn't in this cemetery. It wasn't buried in a coffin with some rotting bones where the book could get wet and muddy and the pages might disintegrate. The journal might to be with Mabel's ghost instead— tucked away safely somewhere in the movie theater.

He took out his phone, but there was still no signal. "Fuck," he whispered to the glowing, useless screen. Dom was about to close the coffin lid and boost himself out of the grave when he heard something that sounded a lot like footsteps.

"Don't turn around." A voice hit Dom like a slap. A guy's voice. "I have a gun pointed at your head."